Alfred Saxelby West

Poems of an Interval

SALZWASSER
VERLAG

Alfred Saxelby West

Poems of an Interval

Reprint of the original, first published in 1863.

1st Edition 2022 | ISBN: 978-3-37500-155-1

Verlag (Publisher): Salzwasser Verlag GmbH, Zeilweg 44, 60439 Frankfurt, Deutschland
Vertretungsberechtigt (Authorized to represent): E. Roepke, Zeilweg 44, 60439 Frankfurt, Deutschland
Druck (Print): Books on Demand GmbH, In de Tarpen 42, 22848 Norderstedt, Deutschland

POEMS OF AN INTERVAL.

BY

ALFRED SAXELBY WEST.

LONDON:

1863.

POEMS OF AN INTERVAL.

THE loppéd tree in time may grow again;
Most naked plants renew both fruit and flower;
The sorriest wight may find release of pain;
The driest soil suck in some moistening shower.

* * * *

No joy so great but runneth to an end—
No hap so hard but may in time amend.

ROBERT SOUTHWELL.

Tombs where lonely love repines,
Glastly tenements of tears
Wear the look of happy shrines
Through the golden mist of years.

R. MONCKTON MILNES.

* * * To Sorrow I was cast
To act and suffer; but remount at last
With a fresh pinion.

LORD BYRON.

CONTENTS.

MISCELLANEOUS POEMS.

SECTION I.

NATIONAL POEMS.

IN MEMORIAM.

SUNDAY MEDITATIONAL VERSES.

MISCELLANEOUS POEMS.

Section II.

METEOROLOGICAL ANNALS.

DESCRIPTIVE PIECES.

SONGS.

MISCELLANEOUS POEMS.

Section III.

LIFE'S DRILLINGS.

POEMS OF AN INTERVAL.

MISCELLANEOUS POEMS.

Section I.

THE RIVER.

A River gushed forth from its grass-strewn source
The soft green hills among,
And murmuring moved in meandering course
The flowery meads along,
And laughing, low lisped its flowing verse,
And rippled its silvery song.

Now it bounds along in bubbling rills,
And the glad vale owns its sway;
Now its drop the thirsty wild flower fills,
As it sprinkles around its spray;
And its heaving bosom joyously thrills
With the boon it bestows on its way.

So stealing thro' sentinel rushes it keeps,
The sloping banks that grace;

While sweetly its sunlit water sleeps,
Where the arching boughs embrace;
And the lily, low bending, softly creeps,
To kiss its shining face.

Soon swelling in stream of wider spread,
No longer it shuns the plain,
But, deepening in its pebbly bed,
It dreams of the distant main;
And it scorns its first shy streamlet thread,
And it cuts the green hills in twain!

Now it pauses to paint the old church tower,
Embosom'd in the glade;
Now winding it skirts some blooming bower,
Where reposes the gentle maid:
And her charms she'll unveil in that languid hour,
When none but the stream dare invade.

It has caught the gay gleams of the morning sun
Slanting down from yon woodland ridge;
And the crimsoned rays when his course is done,
When low flies some buzzing midge;
And the gaze of that blue-eyed little one,
Leaning over the rustic bridge.

Now it courses through Oxford's classic ground,
Where Thame and Isis meet;
Now 'tis twining the castled halls around
Of Windsor's royal seat:

A stately river now ! hill-crowned
By Richmond's fair. retreat.

Then forth it rushes with tidal thrill
To the scene of its ripening fame ;
Bright, eddying, flashing, sparkling still,
Beneath the noon-tide flame ;
For not yet does it dream of the coming ill ;
Tis undimmed by its future shame.

With an emerald circlet of hills that rise
From an undulating plain,
That northward and southward seemed linked to the
In a bright and unbroken chain ; [skies
Thro' their steepled midst its pathway lies,
As it travels toward the main.

(There are rural haunts so pretty and sweet
Our city's streets without,
That lovelior landscapes one may not meet
Half England's isle about ;
And we thitherward wend our willing feet,
And away from the city's rout.

Oh ! picturesque were the spots that here lay
Around thee, thou favored stream !
But our city's stern hand hath swept half away,
Like thine own pellucid gleam.
Still, at eventide yet, we may wander away
Where landscapes, no mean ones, beam).

It has quaffed the dew from yon sloping height,
Near merrie Islington;
It has caught the flood of crimsoning light
Those sweet Surrey hills upon;
With that many arched bridge its clear waters fight,
As they rush impetuous on.

And gay gilded barges deck its brow,
And princely forms are there;
Near stately mansions its currents flow,
The rich homes of the noble and fair.
(But commerce, not chivalry, rules it now,
And hath furrowed deep lines of care!)

So swelling and winding and widening still,
Sped it onward to meet the wave;
Yet the diamond dew of the first green hill
That its infant waters lave—
That it treasured, a tiny and silvery rill—
A tribute to Ocean it gave.

And the wide sea welcomed his gallant son:
"Dear to me are the stores thou dost bring;
Come forth from thy labours faithfully done,
From green haunts where thy sweet waters spring!
I love the fair race-course thou hast run;
To dear Albion's shores do I cling,"

But the river, he sighed for his future fame,
And for trophies costlier far.

Fled the years—and the time of his triumph came;
Now, countless his treasures are,
And o'er the wide world is wafted his name;
Few rivers with his might may compare.

And that mistress-city is the monarch's Queen,
Where the vessels come and go,
As he rolls those ship-lined shores between,
With proud and stately flow;
But riches have banished his silvery sheen,
And darkened his waters now.

We have writ the proud tale of our triumph and might,
With bridges stately and strong,
'Neath whose wide-spreading arches, graceful and light,
Unstayed the black flood flows along;
And stretching away to the wood-crowned height
Are the haunts of the busy throng.

But he sickens between the soiled shores he laves,
Tho' laden with plenty and wealth;
We have made the monarch the worst of slaves,
We have banished his rural health;
And his murky, turbid, and turgid waves
Creep onward in sullen stealth.

So, sickening and reeking with pestilent flow,
That mud-coloured current flies fast;
For it shuns the gay gleam of the woodland glow
On its once shining water cast;

To hide in the heaving billow now
That river polluted runs past.

But the wild waves curl into crested foam!
And roars forth the angry main:
"Return, dark flood! to thy reeking home,
Nor my bright blue bosom stain;
Thy treasures alone o'er my depths shall come;
But thy waters—back, back again!"

So backward the putrid river recoiled—
As the salt sea-tide rolled on—
To haunt the dense spot that its depths had soiled,
Led forth by the crescent moon.
And he sware that the spoilers should soon be spoiled;
He would work his vengeance soon!

But the clear drops cling to the green hill-side,
Where the upland zephyrs play;
For they fear to lose their maiden pride.
But soon, falling in silvery spray,
They are borne to the bounding river wide;
Ah! changed indeed are they!

And is it not thus on life's swelling stream?
We but bathe in childhood's glow,
Enjoy a brief moment its innocent gleam,
Then are swept to soiled channels below!
Tho' with honor and riches our pathway may teem,
Clear water no longer we know.

Our city once, wearied with toilsome hours,
Reclined on her river's breast,
And its clear depths mirrored her moonlit towers,
In hues of soft silver drest;
But where the dark stream estranged now lours,
Her image no longer shall rest.

For the Thames has locked up his liquid sheen
In some rural solitude,
Far away in those woodland valleys green,
Where nothing impure may intrude;
Or 'tis buried beneath that mass unclean,
From the gaze of the city crowd.

For he *will not* reflect the scene of his shame
On his blackened bosom more;
And he *cannot* mirror those marks of his fame,
As they anchor near the shore.
But his wrath he yet fans to a fiercer flame,
On that city ere long to outpour.

Oh! then, ere his vengeance forth be hurled,
Appease we our river king!
At once be our banner of prudence unfurled;
So —disarmed of his pestilent sting—
The commerce and riches and might of the world,
Still to him their glad trophies may bring.

Oh! for the dew-gems shining and sweet
With the breath of the breezy morn,

That shall flow undimmed at our city's feet,
From the fields of the ripening corn!
To the pent-up toil-worn sons of the street,
Like incense from Paradise borne!

From the upland slopes, from the gentle meads,
From the verdant valleys gay,
Rife with the music of rustling reeds,
In those quiet nooks far away,
Where the waters come winding thro' willowy weeds,
With the scent of the new-mown hay!

O London, upwake from thy torpid sleep,
Stand proudly forth on high;
Be mirrored again where thy river runs deep
In the light of a smokeless sky;
Nor longer let night her mantle keep
About thee, when day draws nigh.

And, Londoners, see to the source of your fame,
To the cause of your might and wealth;
Preserve, oh preserve it from further shame;
Restore it its rural health!
So its tide shall still bear ye the rich costly stores
Of the ships from all countries known.
And its currents, fresh from soft sylvan shores,
Shall waft ye sweet dews of your own.

HYMN TO MORNING.

ATHWART the orient sky
Yon crimson bars
Are slow withdrawn;
Heaven's gates wide open fly:
Past paling stars,
On floods of light, in her celestial cars
Rode Maiden Morn.
O Maiden Morn!
Sweet child of Heaven thou art,
'Mid the celestial host of Chaos born!
Thou com'st to earth's poor wearied ones forlorn
Fresh vigor to impart.

Soon fled with sore affright
The spectre-guards of Night;
Scared at so sweet a sight,
Far off they fled—

Or with a strange delight
Methinks half blushed they bright,
And 'neath a curtain draped with burnished red,
Abashed, cowered crouching toward their western bed,
Then vanished quite!

At thine appearing
O Maiden Morn!
Nature laughs out with glee
In gladsome harmony;
Her gayest garment wearing,
Smiles forth in dew-gems to adorn thy way—
Or are they tender drops of grief that fall,
Tears for thy transient stay?—
Meet incense-gems for the celestial Hall,
And borne by thee away.

But Nature dries her tears,
A livelier aspect wears,
And hastes to work in her accustomed way;
And man his burden bears,
His load of daily cares;
But no such glee he shares,
Tho' mourned less, more he feels thy transient stay.

He lays his burden on the lap of Night,
While on her ebon floor,
In sleep's unconscious curtain mantled quite;
His griefs and pains awhile all hid from sight,
Out Memory's close-barred door.

But short that sweet reprieve from human woe,
Night's calm unruffled time!
Gloom—the dark shadow burying gloom—must go;
See ye not now afar the daylight glow?
List to the matin chime!

But ere ye take your burdens back again,
And gird your armour on,
Pause ye; for lo! upon
The far-off confines of the eastern main,
On those faint streaks of dawn,
An Angel rideth. Keep earth's foes at bay!
Let sin's stern conflict for a moment stay!
For the celestial messenger make way;
'Tis Maiden Morn!

She comes with vial of renewing life,
To nerve thee for the strife!
She comes with hope's exhilarating cup
To rouse thee up.
Drink from her goblet bright ere she depart;
Drink! then go forth to fight with freshened heart.

Night only stills dark woe's tempestuous seas,
That, chafing, lash man's breast;
There lie they, shrouded 'neath her shadowy trees,
Deep, dim, below her sable canopies,
Like Stygian pools at rest.

But thou, O Maiden Morn!
At thine appearing, archest them with light,

Beams from bright bowers of Eden by thee borne;
Thou flingest hope's gay bow
O'er the black floods below;
And streams of sorrow flow,
All bathed in amber glow,
Spray-fringed with diamond drops, one sheet of silver white.

But brief that fairy gleam!
Earth's woe-fiends wait without to lash the stream;
Day-storms are rolling near!
Her thunder-peals fall louder on the ear,
Her winds, let loose, in maddening fury fly,
And the now placid stream shall soon swell mountain [high.
And thou! thou canst not stay,
For Heaven's fixed mandate summons thee away;
The opposing forces wait in dread array;
Thou could'st not live amid that dull red glare:
But man, refreshed by thee,
A hero in the strife may be,
The victor's laurels wear.

Go, early Morn, thou hast well performed thy part—
Poured healing oil in many a wounded heart,
Girt the weak warrior with celestial might—
And now thou must depart.
The fresh-keeled ship shall safely ride the storm;
The soldier, mailed, shall face the foeman form,
Nor dread the coming fight.

Hark! there's a whisper in the dewy air;
'Tis borne, O man, to thee.
Oft it has come before; but ah! take care;
This may not always be.
'Tis a soft zephyr from a sunnier clime,
An Eden-breath on these sered wastes of time,
Loosed from eternity!

Methinks the miser's gold sits lighter now
Upon his cankering breast;
And care seems clenching less that sad one's brow:
The man of business and the son of toil
More blithesome tread awhile a lighter soil;
While Mammon waits his willing guest;
For ere that heart to him be once more given,
Flits by one angel-thought of God and heaven.

Now riotous pleasure pales, her tapers dim;
They were but made to mollify the gloom.
The untasted viands spread around the room—
The festal board, where glasses half undrained
Or fallen or broken in confusion lie;
By the red wine some costly table stained,
Which e'en perchance may dye
With crimson pool the floor; that some poor fly
Vainly essayed to sip, but touched to die—
With the stale scent that cowers from morning sky—
These are thy wrecks, O foul debauchery!

Here too the lighter revels gay
Die at the dawn of early day;
And when morn's virgin-light
Steals through the shuttered chinks, with sore affright
They flee, or crouch with awe akin to fear.
The faded finery of the ball-room gear
Here strewn, and mirth's late merry reveller here,
Half tired with pleasure's stay, yet, at its close,
Half grieved that she must haste away;
Some gentle maid (whose sparkling eyes, beneath
That flowery circlet, gleamed so gay
But one brief hour ago,
Now drooping, half inclined to close)
Wearied and sighing for repose,
While her tired head, no matter where, she'd lay,
Bids them take off her wreath.

Thus does voluptuous pleasure flee
At holier glance of thee,
Sweet Maiden Morn!
While those of more licentious glare
Thy sacred apparition shall so scare,
That, all despairing and forlorn,
They'll madly plunge in woe's unfathomed sea;
Thus revelling night may morning's heart-wound be.

But I would hail thy coming, early Morn!
On bended knee,
I looked where thou should'st soon the East adorn;
And, through yon parting panoply of cloud,
I saw heaven's portals slow withdrawn,
And 'mid a shining throng, a white-robed crowd,
I gazed on thee;
While all below hung chill raw mist, and grey,
A brilliant beam shot thro' heaven's door ajar,
Past confines of Aurora's waning star;
It kissed the snow-peaks, thrilled the mists to
light;
And lo! on crimsoned steps, a gorgeous sight!—
Like ladder Jacob viewed with fond delight—
There trod, triumphant conqueror of the Night,
The Maiden Morn.

Yea, for thy coming would I humbly wait
On bended knee;
Nor shamed by Nature-shapes inanimate,
Out of the fulness of a grateful heart—
While kindling fires of love up fresh should start,
A brief and transitory ray,
Meet incense—I would dew-gems weave,
That thou might'st, Maiden Morn, receive,
And bear away
To heaven's Eternal King, poor gift from me.

Alas! but brief indeed
That human freshness of earth's infant day!

As if, 'scaped through those doors, that open stood
When thou and thy bright train descended,
From myriads seraph-harps had blended
In one entrancing tone a golden flood
Of thrilling harmony,
That swept the enraptured sky,
And on our wondering world in falling cadence lay,
To die away.
Thus, early Morning! thou
And all thy treasures are but fleeting things
(Fledged, as the Poet says, with silver wings);
All, all depart again.
For not yet heaven on earth can reign,
Nor happiness be perfect now;
Thou art but in kind mercy sent,
To mitigate man's punishment,
Daily to soothe, to strengthen, and to cheer,
Thou comest here.

But oh! shall dawn the day,
When in one blaze of light,
All the celestial halls wide open thrown,
Through every jewelled gate
In awful state,
An inconceivable array—
A countless throng
Hymning immortal song
A myriad host of angels bright
Shall scare away for ever vanquished Night,
No more a Queen on earth's domains to be;

While He, the great I Am, Ancient of days,
Triumphant riding 'mid those shouts of praise.
To earth shall once again be borne,
Not as a criminal to die,
But as a King to reign ;
While Sin and Sorrow from before Him fly,
Far off in death's deep dismal swamps to lie,
Below that clear, unclouded canopy
Where thou shalt ceaseless stay,
Nor haste away.
For Time shall then be dead,
And all the new creation born
Shall to eternity in deathless splendour lie
Beneath an undimmed lustre shed,
A fadeless glow that shall no more pass by,
Of one Eternal Morn.

"CHILDISH THINGS."

DEDICATED TO

THE EDITOR OF THE "CHEAPSIDE INDEPENDENT."

"We recommend the author ..... to put away childish things."—*Cheapside Independent.*

"Go—if thou art now a man—forget
The simple lays that childhood sings;
With riper intellect, oh let
Thy pen disdain such childish things!
In copious garb of language fine,
Go, veil thy heart's deep murmurings;
Out mystery's caves thy thoughts may shine,
To those who scorn such childish things."

Ye need not bid me change my strain;
My thoughts in newer channels pour;
For oh! I ne'er can know again
The muse that taught me song of yore!
Yet as she mounts her upward track,
Bright gleams angelic back she flings,
Nor manhood's sterner lays shall lack
All remnant of those "childish things"!

To love-tunes mild I swept the string—
The gentle look, the tender glance,
Soft wooings of the maiden spring,
In visioned bowers of gay romance—
Of these the world has heard enough;
Her harp boasts louder, loftier strings;
She's growing far too old and rough
To care for these—such "childish things"!

The smile that nought but age could chase—
Those loving hearts so fond and true—
The vision of some angel-face,
And bright eyes lit with heaven's own blue—
The cheeks methought not yet should pale.
The buds that must to flowers expand,
That fell disease should ne'er assail,
And crush with cold unsparing hand—
But time has proved such fancies vain;
A truer, sadder tale he brings;
And I must now to newer strain—
Must lay aside such "childish things."

The friendships years but tend to bind—
The loves that still sincere remain—
The joys that could not leave behind
One tinge of grief, one throb of pain—
But o'er these cloudless climes of bliss
Soon cold distrust its shadow flings;
And surely time has taught me this:
That these, they were but "childish things."

Come, satire! mould me; so I scoff,
Mock, in maturer murmurings,
At those young warblings, all put off,
Those most unmanly "childish things"!
Come, vigour! train the weak young flower—
Can buds e'er boast of sweets or grace?
Can poesy please, if lacking power?
Those taints of earlier growth displace;
The noontide plant needs noontide rains.
To morn's young bud morn's dew-gem clings;
So mental growth boasts stronger strains,
And lays aside such "childish things."

No; gentler love and cheerfulness,
Meek virtue and her graces mild,
Simplicity and tenderness—
These are all warblings of a child!
Vice, dark ambition, power, and wealth,
The pride, the pomp, the state of kings—
Sure these are signs of mental health.
These the proud lays that manhood sings!
The widening river brackish grows;
It lacks the freshness of the stream;
And where thro' crowded haunts it flows,
What knows it of its woodland gleam?
So sered ones, versed in worldly truth,
That soiled their young heart's purer springs,
They cannot share the spells of youth;
They scorn them, deem them "childish things."

But ere I tear my heart away,
O let me pause, recal once more
The gentle spirit of each lay;
Those poor, weak, "childish" ones of yore!
Nor bid me quite despise the muse,
Who long since spread her silver wings,
But dropped a few ethereal hues,
Poor relics of those "childish things"!
But out the old tower of the past,
Like tone of silver bells, there rings
Sweet sound, that shall in memory last,
Of dear-loved, short-lived "childish things."

THE PROGRESS OF LIBERTY.

SPEED on, speed on, thou mighty river!
Though narrow yet thy channels be,
Lo! they are widening, widening ever,
To merge in one vast shoreless sea.
Flow on, flow on, thou swelling river!
What though thy depths be shallow now,
Lo! they are deepening, deepening ever,
As on, unstayed, thy waters flow,

Once but a little tiny fountain,
Thou pouredst forth from slavery's sod;
Didst pierce the depths of error's mountain—
Great gift of an all-gracious God!
At first in lap of bygone ages,
A small, thin stream, bright trickling on—
Steep, rugged, bare, those earlier stages,
Till poured advancement's plains upon.

Then despots vain thy pathway stopping,
Those swift and shining currents stemmed;
Their barriers thy fierce floods o'ertopping,
Their thrones in ruin soon o'erwhelmed.

And democrats that dared disturb thee,
And tear thee from thy channelled way,
Too soon found out they could not curb thee,
Nor thine o'erflowing waters stay.

And thou art wider now, and deeper;
And thou art spreading, spreading fast;
Those rocks—thy guardian laws—grow steeper,
More firmly are around thee cast.
But thou art narrow yet; on speeding,
Pass those grim heights that frown on thee—
Those banks that bar thy way receding;
On, to the everlasting sea!

On, past where minds grow rank, polluting
Thy stream with error's sewer-stain—
Thy pure flood these but just diluting,
Soon art thou clear and bright again.
Not yet, prepared by Wisdom's harrow,
Yon fields of mind can bear thy sway;
Thy present course at best but narrow,
On every side embanked thy way.

Not till man's mind—a new creation—
For right, and right alone, be free,
Shalt thou spread over every nation,
E'en as the waters fill the sea.
God's gospel-grace, Heaven's great glad tidings,
On these thy future sway shall lie;
There shall be fixed thy firm abidings;
No boundaries but eternity!

SONG TO A RIVER.

I 'D bid thee bear for me, O river!
Weaved into spray,
And swiftly to my love deliver
Upon thy way,
One drop of Cupid's soft spring-shower,
Consigned to thee,
A gem to grace my budding flower,
A gift from me.

But thou'lt not pause, thou restless river!
Thou'rt so proud now;
To Commerce patron and conniver,
So busy thou!
With all thy rank and high position,
Thou brook delay!
Thou'dst scorn so trifling a commission—
Well, flow away.

I could not send thee, muddy river!
I trust thee! no;
I'd be ashamed of thee, its giver,
Thou'dst soil it so.

I'd rather carelessly go throw it
On dusty shelf;
She'd scorn to wear, or e'en to know it—
I'll go myself.

Yet fain one thought of her would ride on
Thy murky way,
And near her, borne the ebbing tide on,
Itself should stay;
She'd view thy wide arm seaward wending,
And muse on thee;
Then her thought on thy breast descending
Mine, with it in sweet union blending,
Would kiss for me.

WINTER EVENINGS.

Come, all put books away;
Read through the live-long day,
Study when best you may;
But now, the hours of labor done,
Homeward returns each weary one,
To mirth and comfort shall they come;
Be ours a bright and cheerful home!

Come, girls, put work away;
Let 's work the whole day long,
But round our fireside's evening ray
Be ours a merry throng.
Our books and work all stowed away,
We'll find such pleasant things to say!
At romping, gladsome games we'll play,
And crown old time with laurels gay
Of jest, and dance, and song.

Let sweet music's strains be heard,
Trilling with harmonious sound
Many a sweet and time-stored word
That in our heart is found;

Dreams of dear-loved voices gone,
Chords that grief-wrung hearts inspire,
Songs breathed by some absent one,
Heard at years-past winter's fire.

Or does hope with gentle hand
Lead us with some livelier air
On, as unprepared we stand,
Some future bliss to share?
Does that clear-toned voice delight?
Do those gentle features charm?
See we paths by her made bright,
Pleasant, happy, sweet, and calm?

Gentle maiden, cease thy spell,
Lest we dull and dreamy grow;
Clear the room, aye, clear it well!
Let the gayer notes forth swell;
Gaily, blithely dance we now;
Wilt thou, fair one, dance with me?
Wilt thou now my partner be?

Friends in pour—they're from next door—
Friends arrive from over the way—
Nimbly tread we the carpeted floor,
Be this our meeting gay!
Heap on the coals! On the snow-clad moor
The cold may hold its sway,
But we'll banish him quite from our close-barred door;
Then merrily dance away!

UNDECIDED.

I KNOW a maiden coy and sweet;
I know a maiden blithe and gay;
I know I love them both to meet—
Both favorites they.

Sometimes I sigh to gain the one,
Yet loth to leave the other too;
One maiden mine—the other gone—
What should I do?

If fate should bid me choose to-day,
And one to be my wife receive,
The coy and sweet—the blithe and gay,
Which should I leave?

They're two fair flowers; then are they not
The rather fitted to entwine?
Perplexing thought, torment me not!
Let Time divine.

Let him distil his severing dew
Of centred, isolated love,
Weave o'er my heart his wisest hue,
Preceptor prove.

In days gone by, we swept our youthful hearts,
And cast aside as worthless in the dust,
A mass of fancies, thoughts, and young conceptions;
For the world said they were not worth the keeping.
Have none found treasures some had dropped unknown
Amid that heap of rubbish? Yea, they have;
Pearls have outshone 'mid dust-heaps of the past;
The thing despised concealed the treasure rare,
But others shared the profits, grasped the gem.

Yea, e'en the naked dust is nature's child,
And not to be accounted dross; she rears it
For future form, a fair and pleasing thing.
And am not I—nay, are we not all dust?
And shall we not be so again ere long?
But does no treasure mingle with the mass?
Aye! One shall find, and snatch the shining jewel
From out the putrid heap, to deck His realms,
To stud heaven's fields with spangled treasures fair;
Poor dust below, but shining dew-drops there!

CENTRED STARS.

COMPOSED FOR THE ISLINGTON YOUNG MEN'S CHRISTIAN BENEVOLENT SOCIETY.

Not one arched sheet of liquid light
Is mantling spread o'er Nature's sky,
That gilds the glowing noontide bright,
Or pales when star-guards watch on high;
But one grand orb of splendour-blaze,
That scares night's cowering shades away,
And through the dusky morning haze
High towers, the pomp, the pride of day:

And, when withdrawn a little while,
Night's myriad lesser lights are sent
To gleam amid the gloom till dawn,
And speck the shadowy firmament,
She, chief of all, Night's silver Queen,
Then stars of more and lesser grace,
Whose centred orbs fair stud the scene,
Each in its own appointed place.

'Tis moral night now reigns below,
For sin's sad gloom dyes all around:
And shades of suffering, want, and woe
Their homes in this fair world have found.

Not yet rolls on the perfect day;
Far off the dawn is halting still,
And Right's triumphant chariots stay,
Nor chase off yet earth's reigning ill.

But God appoints Him lesser light;
Each work of charity is His star
To shine amid the shades of night,
Where sin, distress, and sickness are;
Not to spread sheet-like o'er the sky,
But each a centred orb to glow
(For indiscriminate charity
Effects more harm than good, we know).

Oh, there are noble works abroad,
To aid the needy sons of toil,
And right instruction to afford
To infant outcasts on life's soil!
To rescue them from jaws of crime,
A pure and pious training give;
To make them good men in their time,
And teach them honorably to live.

O Britain! what a future thine!
Thy ripening sons to good inured,
How bright thy unfolding page shall shine!
Thy liberties how well secured!
What patriots, fired with heartfelt zeal,
Shall guard thee in the strife to come,
And bravely watch o'er Britain's weal—
Their prized religion and their home!

Sure ignorance slow shall melt away,
And want and woe diminish fast,
Till comes the messenger of day,
And earth's worst hours of night be past!

These are bright lustrous stars that shine;
And men inspired by God there are
Who carry on this work divine,
Its trials, its successes share.
Yea, e'en the noble of our land,
Men of exalted station high,
Have stooped to lend a helping hand
To heal deep scars of penury.
For these no fleeting hero-fame;
A brighter, greener laurel theirs!
An undimmed crown each soon shall claim,
E'en now a deathless wreath he wears.

Let then *our* little work be viewed,
Compared with these, but faint and small,
A star of minor magnitude—
'Tis well to be a star at all.
Yet we, methinks, have too our work;
'Tis ours to search out and to know
Where want and silent suffering lurk;
There lies our field, to these we go.

There is a secret shame that feels
A blush its naked want to show;

There 's many a decent garb conceals
A cankering breast of withering woe ;
There 's many a house to outward look
Appears respectable and clean,
That the unthinking world ne'er took
To be sad haunt of hunger lean.

A daughter of glad days gone by,
Whom poverty with age o'ertakes,
Her parents dead, no succour nigh,
Soon chill distress its victim makes ;
Far too infirm for rougher toil,
Unused to mingle with the low,
Taught from the vulgar to recoil,
What shall she do, whom turn to now?

This is a general case, we know,
But one we cannot call untrue;
To many like to this we go—
Sure, sure, our labours here are due!
And though but little we can give,
Though 'tis a trifle we accord,
If by our aid they happier live,
There is our work, there our reward.

We are but young, support we need
From those who more of influence have;
And funds, and other aid, indeed
We still from all kind friends would crave.

We are but weak; your prayers we ask
To Him who for the work anoints,
And strengthens for the appointed task
These stars of His, these centre-points.

Only awhile to shine; for lo!
The night already wanes away;
Far off faint streaks increasing glow;
Sweet, welcome harbingers of day!
Meanwhile let each one to his star—
The sad go soothe, the poor relieve;
Remembering "'tis more blessed" far
On earth "to give than to receive."

Soon shall the Sun of Righteousness
Arise in all His saving might,
And sin and sorrow and distress
Shall vanish with the expiring night.
Then shall these poor night-stars grow dim,
For He their Sun shall shine on high,
And heaven and earth shall glow in Him,
Throughout one long eternity.

NATIONAL POEMS.

ON THE DEPARTURE OF HER ROYAL HIGHNESS THE PRINCESS FREDERICK WILLIAM OF PRUSSIA, JANUARY, 1858.

SHE leaves her native land to-day;
Go, Britains! go and hail her;
And as she passes on her way,
Let every loyal subject pray:
May gladness never fail her!

Yea, England's Daughter passes by;
Oh then, with feelings tender,
We will not check the awakened sigh,
But at her parting loud we'll cry,
May Britain's God defend her!

And as she slow rides through each street
Of this her native city,
An eager throng her way shall greet,
Shall bless her with all blessings sweet,
In sorrow, love, and pity.

Yea, pity that she could not stay!
And thus our grief confessing,
We'll share our Queen's distress to-day;
And while we grieve, sincerely pray,
May God go with her on her way,
Her future dwelling blessing!

A people's love, oh! be it near,
When in strange lands abiding;
That she forget not England dear,
And all she loves and honours here.
Then, Britons! give her one last cheer,
While past us slowly riding.

Fair Princess! go; and may that cheer,
Thy land's affection telling,
Be watered by one sorrowing tear,
As loth to part with loved ones here.
Go; but thy country's God still fear—
Pledge of thy love to Britain dear,
In that thy stranger dwelling.

BRITAIN'S WATCHFULNESS.

THOUGH our land delights to see
Peace her island-shores adorning,
Though our country's sons may be
Laborers from the early morning,
Laborers all the live-long day
In the things that make for peace,
Still shall Albion hold her sway,
Nor her far-famed might shall cease.
Let the lands that deem she'll grow
Feebler—let them dare deride her!
Though at peace, they soon shall know
Britain keeps her sword beside her.

'Gainst the subtleties of Might,
'Gainst the tyrant, slyly scheming,
She—the champion of the Right—
Tho' surprised, shall ne'er lie dreaming.
Wakeful still the weak to shield,
Though in lap of peace reclining,
When the oppressors crouch concealed,
Their aggressive deeds designing—

Let one note of peril sound,
And, though peace awhile now guide her,
She 'll prepared for war be found;
For she keeps her sword beside her.

Calmly Britain counts the cost,
And, she'd have her sons all know it,
Though she loves sweet peace the most,
She 'll be willing to forego it.
She 'll to war at once arise,
When the voice of duty calls her,
Up, to succor weak allies;
Ready, yea, whate'er befals her!
Ready, 'spite the words of men,
Men who vainly have belied her;
Aye, and she shall teach them then,
How she keeps her sword beside her.

When unholy powers prevail,
When the tide of truth lies low,
When weak nations quake and fail,
Then we to the rescue go.
Hear it, tyrants! despots, hear!
Now can Albion calm abide her;
But her war-sword yet hangs near,
Sheathed, 'tis true, but still beside her.
And, methinks, the time must come,
When, like those of yore who tried her,
It shall awe, shall vanquish some—
That same sword she keeps beside her.

Warlike sounds from shore to shore
Note ye well; ye know the occasion!
This our answer, nothing more!
To the threat of an invasion:
Slow to arouse though Albion's ire,
When provoked once, 'tis no trifle;
Foemen, hear the echoing fire!
Britain ready makes her rifle.
In the valor of her sons
Calm she feels she can confide her,
And some thousand rifled guns,
Like her sword, lie piled beside her.

For our Church, our State, our Queen,
For the homes ye love so well,
For the quiet village-green,
For the fair and fruitful dell,
For the corn-fields waving white
On the breezy upland's brow—
Oh! for these ye 'd surely fight,
Surely these ye 'll arm for now!
Aye! and Albion's daughters too,
On whose worth she well may pride her,
Who, to guard such treasures, who
Would not wish her sword beside her?

Brood the dark mists o'er the waves,
Spread the nightshades on the sea,
Creeping in the chalk-cliff caves,
Hovering round ye noiselessly:

Quit we now the lighted town,
Climb we to yon furze-hill's height;
On the blackened flood look down
Over Albion's walls of white.—
Mark ye not that far-off flash?
'Tis the watch-light on the shore.
Hush! that sound!—The billow's plash
'Gainst the wood-work, nothing more.

Gaze again; for sure afar
Ships it must be hovering nigh.
Nearer, clearer!—Yes, they are!
Come the foemen, raise the cry!
Flash the news along the wire,
On the heights the beacons make;
England's house is all on fire!
England's sons must up, awake—
Calm ye, maidens, mothers, wives!
Know our land has well supplied her;
And to guard your precious lives
Start they up, that host beside her.

'Mid the crashing of the guns,
Answered by our line of coast,
Every hamlet sends its sons,
Every town pours forth its host.
Hark! our seamen's lusty cheer!
Sails our gallant fleet in sight;
Timely aid! they 're not yet here;
To the death they first must fight.

Calm awhile those gloomy fears;
Think ye past that bar they'll get?—
But the vision disappears;
We are safe, unthreatened yet.

Peers through fog that orb of fire;
O'er the deep the dawn-light swells;
Merrily peal from spire to spire
Dear old England's Christmas bells;
Wake secure to mirthful ease!—
Stay, these things one moment cease;
Thankfully, on bended knees,
Hail a Christmas hour of peace.

At the loom, the mill, the plough,
In the city's busy marts,
Sons of Albion labor now,
With secure and thankful hearts.
At our fireside's gladsome glow,
When we keep our festal day,
When the sparkling wine-cups flow—
Pledge of peace—be this our lay:
Let truth, commerce, freedom spread
O'er all nations, wider, wider,
From the lap of Albion shed,
While her sword lies sheathed beside her!
But let tyrant nations know—
All whoe'er shall dare deride her—
Britain still can face the foe;
Sword and rifle lie beside her.

BRITAIN'S PEACE.

A TRUCE for thee, my native isle!
Thou hast driven the foeman back;
Rest, Albion! on thy sword awhile,
Rest from war's rude attack.
For the clanging din of arms has ceased;
Thou hast stayed war's wasting tide;
From gallant deeds awhile released,
Rest thee thy sword beside.
And while the crafty foe repair
Those well-aimed injuries,
Rest thee in peace; but oh! take care
Thy sword beside thee lies.

Let busy hum of commerce sound
Along thy wave-washed shore;
Let fruitful arts of peace abound;
Go, reap her golden store.
Thy fair fields fill with smiling corn,
Where the laughing streamlets glide,
And the mill goes round in the busy morn,
Or rests in the hot noon-tide.

Let joy and mirth thy glad homes fill;
The strife now past forget—
But keep thy sword beside thee still,
For thou may'st need it yet.

O Albion's sons! secure enjoy
Your freedom, nobly won;
In arts of peace your time employ,
Your island-haunts upon.
In ripening field or busy mart
Be now your labours blest;
But when up fresh the foemen start,
Arouse ye from your rest;
Away from the factory's giddy whirl,
From the matchless marts of trade;
And the blood-stained banner of Right unfurl,
And unsheath the gleaming blade!

But a truce for thee now, thou mighty land!
Awhile by thy sword recline;
While peace still sheds her transient smile,
'Neath her sweet halo shine.
But oh! when the war-fiend stalks abroad,
And gleams in his dull red light,
Then gird on again thy glistening sword,
Thy well-worn armour bright.
Where freedom languishes opprest,
Where'er earth's weak ones fight,
Go, give to those down-trodden peace and rest;
Defend the threatened Right.

The day shall come when the conquered foe
Shall wake to war no more;
When unclouded the sun of peace shall glow,
Upon the unruffled shore.
Then, away for ever with sword and spear,
Nor weapon of war retain;
But *now*, rest thee, and be thy sword still near;
For soon may'st thou need it again.
'Tis a truce for thee now, thou mighty land!
For the foe is driven back;
And thy sons shall rest on their native strand—
But they rest with their glistening sword in hand,
Prepared for each fresh attack.

BRITAIN'S WELCOME.

THEY touch to-day a sweeter soil,
A country valued long,
That cheered them 'mid their cruel toil,
To suffer and be strong.
In unchecked glee they kiss the strand—
Proud, far-spread freedom's hem—
Thus, Britons! honor they our land;
Shall we not honor them?

To guard their rightful sovereign, they
Their time, strength, talents gave;
And sought to point the safest way
His failing throne to save.
Ten years of chains and suffering,
In cold damp dungeons laid—
'Twas thus their perjured traitor-king
His faithful sons repaid!

But—shamed at length by one loud cry
Of horror and disgust
From all the civilized nations nigh—
In *fear and chill* distrust

He sent each from his living grave,
An exile weak and wan,
To western climes across the wave,
A proud, tho' injured man!

They could not honor sovereignty,
All faithless to its trust,
With perjured vows and cruelty
That stained their native dust.
They reverence one, a milder sway,
A holier diadem!
Our Queen and country honour they—
How shall we honor them?

Boldly and bravely 'scaped away
From unjust exile drear—
Britons! they tread our shores to-day;
Let's bid them welcome here.
We may not share their sufferings sad,
That racked each fainting frame;
But we may aid to make them glad,
Who here for refuge came.

Thank Heaven, 'tis not our lot to know
Those martyr-trials sore;
But we may, by our welcome, show
We prize our freedom more.
"Welcome, the noble and the brave,
The hoary and the wise!
Welcome, who nobly strove to save,
To stay, their nation's sighs!

Welcome, who for their country shared,
Endured, the martyr's woe!"
Thus be our greeting strain prepared;
Let 's forth and greet them so.
Stay, Britons! first kneel thank that God
Who freedom's seeds had sown,
To upshoot at length, and grace the sod
Ye proudly call your own!

Then rise, your hearts with love imbued,
While far the sound shall ring;
Go forth, and give in gratitude
A nation's welcoming!
Defiant of the tyrant might
Of Europe's lawless kings,
We shield the Right, and to the Right
We give our welcomings.

England ne'er welcomes vice and wrong;
She 'd scare these from her land:
The man of crime must bear the thong,
It is his righteous brand.
She welcomes those who 've suffered long
In guarding freedom's gem;
For these her bards shall tune their song;
Her sons shall welcome them.

Then, by that liberty ye know,
Their wounded hearts go heal;

And to her tried defenders show
The sorrow Britons feel.
Yea, by the freedom of our state,
The tyrant-tide to stem,
We 'll kindly greet the exiled great,
And gladly welcome them.

BRITISH LIVES.

VOLUNTEERS' SONG.

"The last thing a Volunteer would do would be to die for his country."—*Common Saying.*

No, no! we do not wish to die!
We 've far too much we value here;
Where is *our* dungeoned patriot's sigh?
Where is the tyrant rule *we* fear?
Our laws are mild, our blessings great,
Our homes in peaceful freedom lie;
Who British lives would underrate?
No, no! we do not wish to die.

Aye, but these lives we value so,
And deem too dear to throw away,
We cannot quietly forego,
Nor yield them up to tyrant sway.
Let then the foeman dare to come—
Let Albion dear endangered lie—
We 'll guard as one our island-home,
And hold it as our own—or die!

No, no! we do not wish for war;
Peace is our watchword, peace our aim;
For peace united thus we are—
We do not covet warrior-fame.
O'er gentle green slopes, thick with corn,
And fruitful valleys, as to-day,
Bright with no sabre-flash, may morn
Gleam forth, or eve-tints wane away!
Aye, but that peace we value so—
Too costly count to cast away—
We 'll ne'er submissively forego,
Or barter to some servile sway.
Let then the foeman dare to come—
Let Albion's land endangered lie—
At every cost we 'll guard our home,
And hold it to the last—or die!

We care not conquests new to make,
We seek no territorial gain;
We 'll fight for no mere fighting's sake,
We would, as now, at peace remain.

Yet, though at peace, prepared we stand,
And vow, with no impassioned cry,
We 'll guard as Britons guard their land.
And live as Britons live—or die!
Yes, though at peace, prepared we stand,
And vow—'t is no impulsive cry!—
We 'll guard, as Britons guard, our land,
And live as Britons live—or die!
Should foemen menace then our shore,
For Albion, e'en if death be nigh,
We 'll give, when we can give no more,
That last, best gift, our lives—and die!

LINES

ON THE LAMENTED DEATH OF HIS ROYAL HIGHNESS THE PRINCE CONSORT, *December* 14, 1861.

WHAT foemen rash, defiant in their daring,
Unthwarted up yon winding stream shall sail—
Cruel of purpose, obstinate, unsparing,
Flushed with success, and certain to prevail—
From seaward piercing e'en the land's core, bearing
Swift course to inmost citadel of all,
The central jewels from their setting tearing,
Rich with the spoil that to their lot shall fall?

"None! 'twould be madness—folly, e'en the brooding!
Fleets line our coast, and wall our rivers well;
Forts, like grim teeth, set firm to clench the intruding."
So from our ranks the shouts of safety swell;
And so, where Thames, secure in rural beauty,
Flows tranquil on, we plant our standard fair;
There centres each true patriot's love and duty,
A nation's proudest hopes and chiefest care.

Yet on these heights, in inmost area lurking,
Dread foes have been—the emissary first,
And then the master! each so subtly working,
A *stricken people* hear at once the worst.

Nay, not the worst! our losses scarce half counted,
The bleeding of the wound but just begun—
Who knows to what that influence lost amounted—
The honored debt that at our hands he won?
Not war's impulsive acts a hero crown him;
Slow the uprearing of his fame has been;
Loved more and more by whosoe'er have known
him,
E'en dear to hearts of myriads never seen.

'Twas on the fairest pages of the nation
His name was writ, where Art and Science lie;
Patron of learning! Prince of civilization!
A treasured friend of true philanthropy!—
Successfully discharged his sacred duty—
The Gift he won from England to repay;
His monument—the value of that true tie
Alas! so sudden snapt on that sad day!

Not what he was, so princely in his bearing—
Not what he said, so full of ease and grace—
Our noblest aims and highest interest sharing,
His work scarce finished, who shall take his place?
When on that mournful morn we heard the knelling
That told a great career had reached its end,
Who felt no sudden void, no heart-rebelling,
As tho' at loss of some long-cherished friend?

Kneel, Royal Lady! we too around thee kneeling,
At humble distance, by the selfsame tomb,

Would share thy grief, till heavenly comfort stealing
Shall penetrate again a nation's gloom.
Alas! how poor our strength, how unavailing!
What battlements can bar that foeman's track—
Those royal walls successfully assailing?
Not all a nation's might could keep him back.

Peace! 't was no foeman in that castle standing,
That fleets and forts have failed to drive away:
'T was but a Higher Potentate, commanding
One, who, we feel, was willing to obey.
Peace! 't was a messenger of love, to sever;
See, to a nobler court our Prince he brings—
Where all alike reign kings and priests for ever,
There, in that palace of the King of kings!

THE TWO MESSAGES.

JANUARY, 1862.

ROUND the rough rocky coast the roused storm-wind
    is goading
And lashing the billows that sullenly roar;
While the hearts of the islanders sink with foreboding
Of far fiercer tempest awaited ashore.

Gloomily over the waves were descending
The chill twilight mists of the brief winter day,
While the sky frowned with marks of the tempest
    impending—
Fit type of the gloom o'er the nation that lay!

But a ship cut those night-shades that wrapped us
    in sorrow!
Silently speeding its course from afar—
Though we still, all ignorant, distrusted the morrow,
And pictured dark phantoms of carnage and war.

All armed to the teeth, with her sword old and gory,
Britannia, prepared for the worst, waiting stood;
Her might, was it glorious? How empty that glory!
How poor to console for the shedding of blood!

What hearts through the land in their lone homes
were aching,
Who thought on dear forms they might welcome no
more!
For they knew not how brightly the dawn would be
breaking—
That the storm-wind had wafted a dove to the shore.

Blow, blow, winter blasts! speed the ship to our haven;
The anxiously long waited tidings to greet,
Go forth, men! Oh, is it the croak of the raven,
'Mid the throes of the storm, or the dove's cooings
sweet?

Is it peace? Is it war? War? then take our defiance!
We have means, we have weapons, we have men that
can fight;
But scarcely on these will we venture reliance,—
This our strength, that our cause is the cause of the
right.

Hush! joy-bells ring out, fading over the water,
From the towns nestling low, with the wood heights
above!
And sure 'tis no tale, no sad herald of slaughter—
'Tis a message of peace, with its anthem of love!

Is it peace? Peace! then flash the news far on the wire,
That the dawn with its greetings may make myriads
glad:

Let Science and Nature take part in the choir,
That swiftly it flash upon hearts that are sad.

Peace! then echo the sound thro' the midst of the nation;
From the throne to the hovel these tidings proclaim!
Let the people throng thickly to hear the relation:
Is his country at heart, who can grieve at the same?

Our long-honoured statesman e'en Time has been kind to,
And his fame brightened more as his sun sinks to rest,
Shall his heart feel no thrill as he hearkens, to find, too,
His work for his country so peacefully blest?

And she, that high stricken one, mourning so lonely,
Whose sorrow a nation has trembled to see,
She, too, will her people's jöy share in, if only
One pulse-throb of praise from her heart is set free.

The maid—who her absent one's valour relied on,
Should war, cruel war, put it e'er to the test—
Smiles to know that the case she alone need decide on,
That the deep-felt assurance lies locked in her breast.

And mothers and wives—nay, the depth of *their* feeling,
When doubt's galling chain is so sudden removed,
Lies veiled in that chamber whence praises are stealing
To Heaven, for the safety of those so beloved!

Our almost-proved foes we can 'wait—if still liking
At variance to live with their nearest of kin—
Enough; they have cancelled the need of our striking!
Leave time better feelings once more to bring in.

Though the war-spirit brood yet afar on the ocean,
Though the heavings of strife must have time to
decrease,
We Britons can feel but one gladsome emotion:
Glory, glory to God for the blessings of peace!

BRITAIN'S RECORD.

CHRISTMAS, 1862.

What of Albion's sons of toil?
Iron hands and sinewy brow—
Humble tillers of the soil—
Hardy guiders of the plough—
Rude, but honest hearts of oak,
Glowing with true British fire—
Shall they not our praise invoke?
Manly workers, fit to admire!

What of Albion's sons of toil,
Who her teeming factories fill—
Where the gleaming lathe-wheels coil—
Swarms that throng the busy mill?
Proud in labour; prouder far
In their clouded hours of ill—
Strong of will and heart they are,
While their haunts are hush'd and still,
Cold and hungred, famished, lean,
Poor and haggard, weak and faint,
Yet their truest strength is seen
Uttering not their sad complaint;
In their patience firm of will—
Not one riot, tumult, broil—

Strong to suffer, and be still.
History's present page unrolled,
Write, in characters of gold,
This of Britain's sons of toil.

What of Albion's men of crime?
Shades that scare our land to-day,
Strong to awe a little time—
Who withal so weak as they?
What of Albion's sons of crime?
Nay, they are not Albion's sons;
Meshed in vice's densest slime,
They are Satan's shackled ones;
They're no British freemen true.
History's present page unrolled,
Write, in characters of gold:
These—they were a meagre few;
But the myriads are our boast;
Though their heads awhile hang down,
Oh, there's not a nobler host
That a noble land can own!

And their recompense shall come;
Tried, for trust and honor meet;
In the future to become
That which now is incomplete:
Higher in the social scale,
Fit to govern as obey—
Voice all glorious to prevail—
Who a country's strength as they?

Poor the power, if vast the realm,
Tho' a continent be theirs,
Where the strength is at the helm,
But a rot the vessel tears.
All their braggart insults hurled,
All their vain conceit outblown—
Lo! their bubble power has burst.
They aspire to rule the world!
They must leave the world alone,
They must rule themselves the first.
There's a semi-civilised state
Must recross barbarian ways,
Right through war and mutual hate,
Ere made meet for holier days.

Which is nearest to the goal,
Future goal of nations great?
Is it not where strength of soul
Gains the victory over fate?
Where the unsuffering mass condoles,
And a nation's wealth consoles
Those, who've learnt to bear and wait—
Task heroic, truly great,
Fitter far to emulate!
When the present's page is done,
As the record ye unroll,
Read ye there this golden scroll,
Of each suffering British son,
Of their patient fight with fate—
Tumult, rash seditions, none!—
How they bore their lot, and won!

THREE POEMS

In Commemoration of the Arrival and Marriage of Her Royal Highness the Princess of Wales,

March, 1863.

I.

The Three Treasures.

A north-east storm of battle scoured the land
When Albion's bud was young; and at its fury
Her monarch—time enthroned—hung down his head,
And lay awhile obscured beneath the gloom.
But precious spoils—stern Northern hardihood
And naval daring—on that tide of war
Rolled westward, a rich freight, upon our strand;
Seedlings that cast firm root, growing hereafter
A world-famed nation's noblest tree of strength.

Stemmed for a moment by a valiant hand,
Those transient barriers, raised by that first hero,
Again fell powerless—futile, unenduring,
Before the fierce resistless tide of conquest,
Which (*like the sea that scorned imperial power*)

Came on unto its full tide—but its flood
Brought fresh accession from the eastern isle,
When Wisdom, quelling flattery, ruled in Britain,
And reared its trophies side by side with Valor.

Ages passed by; the blossom, hardier grown,
From all its bracing spring-time left its verdure,
And the rich fruit a proud experience brought.
Now once again, a nation, manly grown,
Casts eager eyes towards the little spot
Upon that eastern sea; and once again
The tide sets in—not war's destroying billows,
But tranquil flood, impelled by gentle gales
Of happy peace—and on her summer balm
Wafts from that self-same shore her latest treasure,
The complete measure of the threefold gifts.
With Valor in the van, and Wisdom following,
What fitter climax, gift more meet to rank
In honor equal to those cherished two?
Valor and Wisdom, golden gifts of yore,
Now linked to gentle grace and maiden beauty!

From the isles across the sea,
Where our sailor-hearts were reared,
Came the valor to be feared,
Came the wisdom to be free.

From the land across the sea,
Lo! the latest gift appearing,
Greeted by a nation's cheering,
High-born beauty welcome we.

'Mid the booming of the gun,
'Mid melodious sound of bells,
Hark! a nation's joy-strain swells:
Honor to her! and to *his* son
(Canute and Alfred all in one)!

Honor and happiness to him!
The sun that shone on his young mind,
Though hid death's fleeting cloud behind,
Oh be its cast light never dim!
Oh be his father's goodness there!
Left photographed upon his heart,
That time may never bid depart,
In character that fadeth ne'er!

And be her influence as of yore,
When valor from her native shore
Flourished and ripened, spreading o'er
Our country's richly leavened store—
So spread its blessing evermore!

Oh may their joint lives peaceful prove,
Revered and loved by every class,
All good and wise deeds long to amass!
Duty's rich fruits 'mid flowers of love.

II.

Another Royal English Home.

Home of all English homes the chief,
Of our domestic land the pride,
Oh shine from out thy cloud of grief,
And cast thy mourning garb aside!
Oh be as thou wert once of yore,
Stand forth as thou wert wont to stand—
The centre star upon our shore,
The great example of the land!

Alas! methinks it must not be;
The broken links can no more bind;
That perfect whole we ne'er shall see,
But sundered fragments doomed to find.
Yet from dead flowers that had their lives
Sweet buds of future life may come;
So heaven a new-born treasure gives—
Another royal English home.

Up, Britain! 'mid thy thousand homes,
From thine accustomed quiet start!
Prepare to welcome her who comes,
With glad acclaim of voice and heart.
Be those rich spoils that graced the wreck,
Transplanted to the newer bark;

Be every virtue there, to deck,
'Mid life's drear flood, love's hallowed ark.

Far distant from their firmament
May death and sorrow's clouds long stay,
And only blessings fresh be sent
To add new stores, not take away;
That she, whose loss time ne'er can heal,
Long, long upon her cherished throne
May in her children's children feel
The hopes and joys once all her own!

With proud experience of the past—
Rich soil where such sweet hopes were sown—
A nation's joy, no more o'ercast,
Now rises in all hopeful tone.
Throughout our streets an eager throng,
With lips of greeting full, shall come
And welcome, with glad shouts and song,
Another royal English home.

III.

After the Pageant.

Take down the tinsel and the trappings;
Those shouts prolonged have died away,
A people's deafening cheers and clappings,
Those flashing light-devices gay.

Unroof that arch—to outward seeming
A thing so white and pure and fair!—
A nation wakes, as though from dreaming
A blissful dream, to morning's care.
Those gilded columns, pillars hollow,
Those richly crimsoned planks remove,
Ere tawdry shabbiness can follow,
And time their pseudo-nature prove.
But yet that stern stone bridge now viewing,
One feels a throb of passing pain—
While beauty's wreck the ground is strewing—
To leave all cold and bare again!

It must be so with earthly splendour;
Those joyous outbursts soon fleet by;
Yet well if, like sweet blossoms tender,
To yield a fruitage rich, they die.
A people's grand rejoicings over,
Let joy-seeds 'neath the surface rest,
And common daily life but cover
A calm delight no years molest;
Till flowers of hope and leaves of action
Burst forth to beauty in their spring,
And stores of future satisfaction
Come loaded with rich fruits they bring.

What are the fruits of this proud union
A mighty people joyed to view?—
Two nations linked in fresh communion,
That e'en of old a kinship knew:

A kindly thought of past relation,
Where treasures from one stock we trace;
The valor of a sea-girt nation,
The glory of an island race.

And as one common past possessing,
That each is proud and pleased to own,
So bring the future mutual blessing,
Joint interests ne'er to be o'erthrown!
Links of that chain the nations binding
In one strong phalanx, shore to shore,
Till all in all true brothers finding,
Men learn to hate and war no more.

What more the fruits? A new formed home
From out those grief clouds has appeared;
May the dropt mantle his become
Who knows what made the old endeared.
What fruits? Let's hope a royal line
Of princes Britons long may own,
In whom *his* character may shine,
Who reared in British hearts his throne.
What fruits? We note the monarch cherished,
The truest safeguard of a throne
Preserved (while all around has perished),
For fringed by Freedom's shining zone.
The fruits? Sweet streams of future gladness,
Those bitter floods to flow between,
To lessen more and more her sadness—
Our own beloved, but widowed Queen!

What are the fruits? The harvest cluster,
Far finer than earth's bowers could rear,
Their richest graces, ripest lustre,
Are garnered in a higher sphere.
Of love's pure bond the full completing,
Oh! not to this world's care is given—
Immortal 'mid all earth-hopes fleeting,
They blossom here, bear fruit in heaven.

There, take them down, those bare wood pieces,
That seemed so firm, so fair and strong;
A nation's noble pageant ceases—
Room for the daily city throng!
Those painted planks, those gilt devices
(Though feelings half regretful flow,)
Their part is played, their work suffices,
Their spell is ended—let them go.

In Memoriam.

His Question.

Did she love me or no? Did she love me?
I have asked my lone heart oft before;
And it whispered dark doubts; so I strove me
To brood on its answer no more.

Did she love me or no? Gentle maiden!
Whose bright eyes illumine my lay—
I will ask thee; one brief moment pay, then,
Attention to that I shall say.

When I wooed her, she gladly consented,
And her love-vow she sealed with a kiss;
She has said since she never repented—
Prove, maiden! she loved me, by this.

But the rose-tint burnt in, for the snow-hue
Fell coldly, and clasped her cheek round,
And it scared the blood, wildly to flow through
The swoll'n veins with feverish bound.

And I saw the sad symptoms, and trembled,
For I felt what the ending must be;
But I spoke all in truth, nor dissembled
When I *said that* still faithful I'd be.

Did I love her? I felt that to quit her
Would be to go forth into night,
That no future with her could be bitter,
And no present without her be bright.

Did she love me? She too guessed the ending,
And yet could to-day's joys forego,
And bliss from her own heart be rending,
Because it but bloomed upon woe.

Did she love me, who knew stole a step on
To snap love's slight cord of to-day,
And yet made her own hand the weapon
To tear the brief fastening away?

Did she love, who could calmly go sever
What should have been part of her life,
And could e'en bid it farewell for ever,
Under cloak of dissension and strife?

That for his, or the world's sake, ne'er shrinking
Her own love to sacrifice quite,
She could let him depart from her, thinking
She never did love him aright:

And when love like a poor snow-drop flourished,
That should ne'er know its bright summer day,
Deemed it no more a boon to be nourished,
But coldly could put it away:

And his love—who yet sighed to be with her
When hope fled affrighted away—
Since to-morrowless, bade she go hither,
And leave her unloved too, to-day!

This, then, is my story—dear maiden!
I have told it all freely to you;
Search deep in your own heart, and say then,
Could her love for me really be true?

And if in your maiden-heart seeking,
An echo respond to the same,
And this doubt-tangled story seem streaking
With a ray of unravelling flame—

Oh, then make it brighter and clearer,
So that all to her honor be proved,
And time her sweet memory write dearer,
Who never belied that she loved.

[A friend to whom the above Poem was lent, returned it with the following reply, which is inserted by permission.]

ANSWER TO "HIS QUESTION."

I HAVE searched, I have sought, in the depths of a heart
That in constancy vies throb for throb with thine own,
And an instant reply has arisen, to dart
The death-blow at doubts thou hast anxiously shown.

Sure 'tis one of those questions (too rare, but most sweet)
Never made till the doubt has been charmed into rest;
And the answer, consenting, flies joyful to meet
The secret persuasion long nurst in the breast!

Yet the answer I'll give—for reproof sharp and stern
He deserves, who thus measures a true woman's love;
Who suspects that her heart, once his own, could return,
And indifferent, cold, and inconstant could prove!

Not so; oh, not so! I, a woman, declare
That a woman, once loving, loves on to the last;
A thousand misfortunes may darken the air,
No cloud the blue heaven of her love can o'ercast.

A true woman's love, understand, will consist
In a cherishing, purely unselfish and high,
Which, while worthy the object remains, can subsist
Without your (supposed) indispensable tie.

Be the contract dissolved; scatter each solemn sign—
The registered vow, and the clasp of the hand—
Still no force can compel her to tear from its shrine
The loved image not even stern death can demand.

That *her* heart's love was thine from the first, I perceive
From the reasons that in thy simplicity thou
Hast given for the thought (sure thou did'st not believe)
That her heart was inconstant, untrue to its vow.

When the sad truth to light from its hiding-place burst,
And an Angel-voice ceaselessly called, "Rise, depart!"
With true love that sought *his* best interests first,
She schooled her kind lips for hard words—"We must part."

Yet she knew, well she knew, that the heart all her own,
Whom she now bade return and seek elsewhere for love,
Could boast of a virtue alas! little known;
A constancy firm that no trifle could move.

She foresaw he would cling (as it proved) undismayed
To his treasure, whate'er days to come might unroll—
For this was not a choice from self-interest made,
But a holy affection of soul knit with soul.

She prayed all in vain he would leave her to die—
All more fondly he cherished the sweet fading flower;
For only *one* thought—then undreamt of—that tie
(Heaven-made) to destroy, e'en to loosen, had power.

While believing her heart beat responsive with love,
Ev'ry argument useless he still put aside;
For nothing but misapprehension could move
His soul to believe what his senses denied.

And it came. Was she glad? For his sake, perhaps yes;
So the word re-assuring she would not pronounce,
But locked up her heart, though she longed to confess
That for his sake alone she such bliss could renounce.

Content to be misunderstood by the world,
She withdraws to prepare for her heavenly home;
And as faster the sunstrokes of trouble are hurled,
The riper and lovelier her virtues become.

"Did she love?" Ask again; put it thus: "Does she love,
Now her spirit is free from the cold sleeping clay?"
Her last words were enough the base doubt to romove:
She has carried her love to the regions of day.

You have proved that she loved you while lingering here;
And perhaps not a few preservations you owe
To the watchful affection stored up for you there,
Where the messenger-angels swift fly to and fro.

HEAVENLY TRANSPLANTINGS.

SHE was not framed to linger here,
A child of earth—ah! no;
It was to grace a higher sphere,
I let that loved one go.
But had she been for this world framed,
To tarry long below,
Think you I 'd leave her thus unclaimed,
That thus I 'd let her go?

Should aught else loose Love's golden chain,
Dissolve her sacred spell,
Or sever friendship's bond in twain?
Oh no! this were not well.
But when, too frail for earth's keen bowers,
Faint droop they, weak and low,
We say—they 're trained for heavenly flowers—
And then we let them go.

They go to bloom in realms of bliss,
To deck a brighter place;
They go, the chosen plants of His
Who bought them in his grace.
And yet our souls would seek a share,
Nor part would quite forego;
Would claim them in heaven's garden—there
No more to let them go.

O then, my soul! forbear to grieve,
Nor sigh to keep her here;
For thou that loved one may'st receive
Within some brighter sphere!
But if, in earthly beauty framed,
She had bloomed in bowers below,
Then this lone heart its prize had claimed,
Nor let the dear one go.

MY DREAM.

"I had a dream, which was not all a dream."—BYRON.

I HAD a dream—nay, *this* was but a dream—
A vanished vision in that loved past's sleep,
Viewed once, twice, thrice, in youthful hours of yore!
The fair form that I loved so was beside me,
And I bent over her in tenderness,
And took her hand, and placed it in my own,
All fearful lest my cherished one should flee.
But she arose, methought, and strayed awhile
To join her friends, engaged in converse near.
Then did I seek for her—but all in vain!
The shadow of my dream had parted us.
So I groped after her in fear and sadness;
So lone I sought her, but I failed to find her.
But, waking, days of bliss came—mellowed—faded.

Again a vision wrapped my soul in light.
I roamed, all happy, in a pleasant garden,
Where scenes of beauty basked in sunshine round me;
For the bright orb had gemmed the morning dew,
Tinted the fragrant flowers with colored sheen,
Glowed on the lake, and glazed the green bough-tops,

And wooed the landscape with its cheerful light;
And all created nature beamed with joy;
The cup of life seemed running o'er with glee.
But lo! a storm came on, and all grew dark;
All shrouded lay the landscape at my feet,
Drowned in the gloom the fields, and trees, and
flowers;
They were all round me still, perchance unchanged,
But oh! could they be still the same to me,
Tho' yet amid them? But methought there came
Some form to me, tho' who I could not tell
('Twas well, methinks, the darkness hid it from me),
Who took me by the hand, and forced me out,
Reclosed the gates, and firmly fastened them,
Then vanished; and I stood outside, alone.

Then the gloom rolled away, and all was peace;
More bright the sun shone o'er that cherished spot,
In sweeter rays and clearer than before:
And I—I knew it, though I could not enter.
Where was the comfort for the banished one?
But now more mellow drooped it o'er the hills—
Those last dim boundaries of the spot I loved—
And kissed them, and went by, and all was dark.

Then they unbarred the gates and bade me enter,
And rove there as of yore, now all was dark!
Aye! in the gloom—as if the dear delight
That hovered there 'mid lake and tree and flower,

Had stol'n not off with the departed sunbeam!
So grew I wroth, and said, "I will not enter."
But lo! uprose the moon, and myriad stars
Outshone, and all the old delights appeared
Lit with a sudden, but a softer hue;
Yet to my mind as sweet; they seemed to me
A holy reflex of the faded past,
And I roved 'mid them!
Once again a room;
And she I loved again beside me in it!
'Twas that sweet presence seemed the sunlight there.
Oh, how I loved to bask in that bright face!
But glides the vision on—it must be so,
For joy and sorrow come and go by turns—
At least in dreams—and now the door is closed,
And I without! and yet that cherished one
In brighter lustre fills the room denied me;
More precious though I dare scarce look upon it.
But now they ope the door, and bid me enter.
Is it to mock me that it should be so—
Just to behold the sunlight die away?
They take the jewel out its once dear case,
And leave me there now all is dark and joyless.
But I—why should I linger in it now?
I might as well be in the cold damp street,
In the chill mist-fall of an autumn twilight,
When the rough blast has whirled the dead leaves by.
I will go hence!—But lo! before me rose
The soft full moon of sad remembrance sweet,
And myriad stars of countless moments dear,

That time upbore to glimmer down upon me
From out the fled past's distant firmament;
For memory's moonlight shewed it me once more,
With those dear charms that made it so beloved—
The empty chair—the silent instrument
(But poor comparison with harp of gold
That blends with those celestial hymns of praise!)—
All these I gazed on; but a holier feeling
From heaven, like star-beams, calmly lit my soul;
'Twas there I looked to attain it, and be still.—
Then did I wake to find it—*all* a dream?

DEW-DROPS.

Sweet dew-drop of life's morning dear!
Awhile to glad us given—
'Twas mercy's beam that gemmed thee here,
Then drew thee pure to heaven!

What! would we thou wert left alone,
To glisten long below?
Nay, that same sun that o'er thee shone
Gave thee thy richer glow;

Shed round thee holier, purer light,
And framed thee far more fair;
Then drew thee to the heavenly height,
To shine all spotless there!

CONSUMPTION.

LIFE,—the bright angel nearest to the throne
Of the Almighty Everliving One;
Whose special office, blessed avocation!
Is from the crystal seas that lave heaven's shores
To take up precious drops, and sprinkle them
On myriad worlds that from afar roll round
The blessed seat of their Almighty Maker—
Life had a cherished sapling that she loved,
A maiden young and blithe and beautiful,
Blooming amid the bowers of this our world;
And all the charms that she could lavish on her—
Grace, beauty, health, and fragrance—these she gave her.
Sure life bloomed here in all her zenith brightness!

Now the fallen angel, Death—Sin's minister—
He too beheld, and while he viewed, he envied;
And coveted his hated rival's treasure.
So sent he soon his trusty minister,
And bade him haste, go bring the flower to him.
But lo! Disease, less cruel than his master,
Forebore to pluck at once the tender plant.

He saw and pitied, and methinks had spared,
Had not the tyrant's will proved absolute;
And so he gently placed his iron hand
Upon it, loosening it a little first,
And then a little more; and day by day
The flower bloomed on, though less Life's sap flowed
in it;
The flower bloomed on that he too loved to gaze on;
The flower bloomed sweeter, though from earth more
loosened;
A more celestial bloom it seemed to wear—
As gay-plumed butterfly that soars unfettered
The flower of air—it seemed almost untrammelled,
As if, no more affixed to earthly stem,
Nor needing sap that this low world supplies,
The flower, expanding all her folded leaves,
Would soar unsullied to celestial bowers!

But now so loosened grew she from earth's stem,
That life-blood ceased to flow—the maiden died!
The hues of beauty, brightest at the last,
Grew too unreal for earth, then faded quite.
The flower off-broken, withered, fell to earth;
The last slight thread of stalk, that gently stayed it,
Gave way; the flower fell faded to the ground.

Then Death quick claimed his prize, essayed to sip
The living fragrance that the flower gave up,
To catch the soul that winged its flight to heaven.
But Life stood weeping by her loved one dead—

When He, the Lord of these two angels, came;
He took from Death's stern grasp the life, the fragrance,
And carried it, unmarred, away to heaven;
He left Death just the sered and withered leaves;
And told him he might keep these for a while,
Till He should come and claim them back again,
Re-shape them into lovelier, purer form,
Instil in them the fragrance now removed,
To bloom anew in his unfading bowers,
Where all is life, and Death shall never enter.

ANNIE.

On Receiving her Portrait.

Last eve he gave it me. He would have given
The very form, instinct with gladsome life,
And bid me guard and cherish tenderly—
But that a surer owner than himself
Claimed back the gift, and He—so prodigal
Of favors more than we can e'er deserve—
In that denied me; left me this alone,
And took the living form away from us.
Vain were the murmuring when 'tis Wisdom grants not!

And this is all! The fled past's spreading brightness,
Its joys and happy hours all narrowing here—
Like sun-rays that have floated far and wide,
Converging to one little point, there fixed
For ever—thus did sorrow's fastenings hide
The scenes and happy haunts of that brief day;
And but one narrow streak, one gleam alone,
Stole thro' the darkened chamber of my heart—
This one memento of life's sunny morn,
Which gazing on, brings back its sweets to me—
This little impress here!
And is this all?
Yet 'tis like balm to stay the withering flower,
To keep the rose of spring-time whole and perfect,
So Memory's triumph may be more complete
Against the ruthless, stern destroyer, Time.
All but the life! Nay, not the imaged fabric!
But what of that? The true ideal of it,
Concentred in this little space, and fixed
Unchanged in bloom of an eternal youth!

Say, would that form so fair, if truly real,
And lit with life on bounding, free, and healthful,
Have still remained as I can view it now?
Would nought have dimmed the lustre of the eyes,
Or filled their unclouded blue with bitter tears,
Or changed that soft and sweet expressive glance
To wearied look of care, perchance of wrath?
Would never wrinkles on that calm white cheek
Have grown, the unswaying waves of wearied age?

Oh grieve not too much; for that life ye sigh for,
With all that this is but poor symbol of,
Could ne'er have passed along the plains of time
Unchanged and young, as that you gaze on now
In youthful beauty. Rather joy to know
That a pure spirit, born to blithesome youth,
Should know not age, but in that youthful form
Should bloom awhile upon this changing earth,
Then, young and lovely still, throw off the apparel,
Which, tho' so fair, was earthly after all,
And, in a brighter and a purer garb,
Go in her youth, and stand before her God!

Ye tell me, "Come away! a little scene
Of early love—there 's many a like one yet
In store for thee; and thou wilt soon forget
Or, careless, deem this but a trivial grief,
An unripe fruit, a little broken bud,
Swept down before the raging blasts of time,
That grew to nothing after all." So speaks
The selfish world unmoved.
Aye, come away!
Away, my soul! this is a world of action;
Thou must pass by, nor stand all idly sighing
Beside the grave-stone of the past. Away!
Aye, so I will—but one brief moment more,
One other tear, then will I turn away,
And be as active as ye would desire,
Amid this life's day-duties and its pleasures.

But know for sure, that, tho' I come away,
I close the gate, and gird the spot around
With jealous feeling; there, all safe and sacred,
Enshrined within my heart I'll leave my sorrow,
While memory rears around it such a temple
As shall defy the assaults of time and you.
Then oft from busy scenes of years to come
I 'll turn aside, and enter silent there,
Take off the sandals of a soiling world—
While not the dearest then shall dare intrude
With unbared head—and stand alone beside
This sorrow time shall spoil but of its sting.
And thus this memory of the past shall rest
Enshrined, like saint or angel-vision fair,
Within that fabric fashioned in my soul.
And thus in meditative calm, resigned,
My thoughts shall soar to her, from her to God.
And though the shades of age steal slow upon me,
And time and care deface life's fleeting day,
In memory's shrine shall all come back to me,
The freshness of the youth I spent with her!

There, now I come; the interment is completed,
The fane of youth's sore trial well nigh closed;
Ye may not pierce its portals, but e'en ye
Will mourn the death of beauty, sigh o'er one
In all the young fresh grace of early years
Nipped by disease's chill wind, and laid low,
A flower of zenith beauty. Yet one moment
Bear with me.—Now I come, impatient world!

To joy and sorrow with ye as of yore;
But I will hold the key of this my temple,
To come and go out whensoe'er I please—
I have it, gazing on this portrait here.

SUNDAY MEDITATIONAL VERSES.

The Presence.

SEE COLLECT FOR FOURTH SUNDAY AFTER TRINITY.

The ship sails silent on the sea;
On every side fierce waves rise high—
One round about that ship will be,
Who fills the air, the sea, the sky.

The corn-sheaves rustle on the land
In deep green dells the streamlets sing—
And there, too, One is nigh at hand
To tune the wild note of the spring.

From eastward sullen night steals on,
All dark and treacherous, awful, still—
Who conquering rides the light upon,
Can densest depths of darkness fill.

When all is peaceful, sweet, and calm—
When raging winds or seas are high—
Or dark, or light—the Eternal Arm,
Still powerful to control, is by.

Though sin from Him has lured us far,
If Him we'll seek, He'll seek us too—
Be near us wheresoe'er we are,
And with us whatsoe'er we do.

In peace, in war, on sea, on shore,
O'er waves of ill, in vales of bliss,
Our chosen Guide He'll go before;
For Christ is ours, if we are His.

The River.

SEE COLLECT FOR FIFTH SUNDAY AFTER TRINITY.

"Thou visitest the earth, and waterest it; Thou greatly enrichest it with the river of God, which is full of water."—Psalm, lxv., 9.

How sweet in sultry summer hours,
When all is scorched and parched and dry,
The cooling drops that gem the flowers,
Ere dawn hath crimsoned yet the eastern sky!
Or the refreshing noon-day showers,
From the soft clouds that fleetly fly,
With zephyr-breeze that fans the bowers,
When the meridian sun flames fierce on high!

Down from the green-hill top they come,
In channels deep of moistened earth,
And bubbling quit their infant home,
Hasting to work His will who gave them birth.
In silvery streamlets, see! they glide
By grassy slope and flowery mead;
Now trickling down some steep hill-side,
Now winding, half concealed, through willowy weed.

And green trees grace their shining breasts
With arching boughs that thick embrace,
'Neath whose soft shade the streamlet rests,
Ere onward still its useful track it trace.
And there the bright birds build their nests,
And there their young in safety place;
While towering high, yon hill-top crests
And bounds the valley's intervening space.

Sweet treasured stores! where'er ye glide,
Through ripening corn, or grassy lea,
Ye are the grateful valley's pride,
And the high hills look down approvingly!
And soon to spreading rivers wide
Ye swell, as onward still ye flee;
And man rears up his haunts beside
Your deepening floods that bear his ships to sea.

Our once fair world grew sered and dry,
For sin dispelled sweet founts of love
That Heaven had poured forth from on high,
To water guiltless Eden's hallowed grove.

But God sent down His much-loved Son,
Who reared again the shattered well,
Whence sweeter drops should henceforth run,
And into wider, deeper channels swell.

Those precious drops that Calvary dyed,
Are spreading still in mightier flood;
And they who stand its shores beside
See in its crimsoned depths their King and God.
And, plunging in that healing stream,
The lep'rous stain is washed away,
And rays of Heaven upon them gleam,
To shine still more unto the perfect day.

Channel of grace! sweet sacred flood!
May this thy glad course never fail;
Supply the world with heavenly food,
With holy waters fill the parching vale!
Thy precious source, our Saviour's blood,
Be that each sinner's joyful tale;
Till all earth's erring sons have stood
Upon thy banks; thence shall they sail
Far on thy depths, made pure and good,
To those bright shores thy boundless waters veil.

Grant, Lord! that while through earth it flows
In narrower channels peacefully,
Deserts may blossom like the rose,
And far and wide around its work may be.

And may thy children on its banks,
From deepest stains of sin set free,
By holy lives give grateful thanks,
All willing yield their blood-cleansed hearts to Thee!
So shall they join at length the sinless ranks
That bend before Thy throne continually.

The Landscape.

SEE COLLECT FOR SIXTH SUNDAY AFTER TRINITY.

"Eye hath not seen, nor ear heard, neither have entered into the heart of man, the things which God hath prepared for them that love Him."—1 Cor. ii. 9.

We have seen full many a fair one
Glide about this earth of ours—
Where the heart that hath been ne'er won
By the fresh green trees and flowers?
Who but loves to look on beauty,
Shine and cheer where'er it may?
Dull had seemed mere lives of duty—
Just to fear, and to obey!—

But a kind and loving Maker
Spread our world with scenes so fair,
That each child might be partaker
With Him these delights to share;
And He loves that they should glory
In the works His hand hath made,

Viewing in Creation's story
Wisdom, power, and love displayed.

We have seen in summer splendour
Landscapes stretching far and wide,
Hues of evening, soft and tender,
Mellowing tint the green hill-side;
And the fruitful valleys lying
Where the laughing streamlets glide,
While the silvery shades are dying
In the dusk of eventide.

Some have climbed the snow-peaked mountains,
Towering upward to the sky—
Sat beside cool shady fountains,
Where the parching deserts lie—
Roamed upon the shoreless billows—
Been where polar icebergs rise—
Or have spread their downy pillows
'Neath some sunny southern skies.

Scenes of beauty, scenes of grandeur!
Can ye ever fail to please?
What cold heart that would not wander,
Glad to gaze on spots like these?
Nature! clad in simple beauty—
Flashing in array more wild—
In whatever light we view thy
Charms, they glad each earthly child.

Ye that love the glorious landscape,
Climes more beautiful there are!
Could not that Almighty Hand shape
Lands than these more glorious far?
List! He tells of landscapes brighter
Far than mortal eye hath seen;
Shining in apparel lighter,
Clothed in never-fading green.

Beauteous things on earth we cherish,
Flowers, and trees, are born to fade;
All we love on earth must perish;
Summer flies from winter's shade.
But those beauties are undying,
Mountains time shall ne'er remove,
Vales in rich luxuriance lying,
Landscapes that unchanged shall prove.

Only we must love the Giver,
If such gifts we would enjoy;
So He will from sin deliver
Hearts so stained with earth's alloy;
Hearts that must, to Him first given,
Jesus' righteous garment wear,
Then, apparelled thus for heaven,
He will come and take us there.

The Prayer.

SEE COLLECT FOR TWELFTH SUNDAY AFTER TRINITY.

"No good thing will He withhold from them that walk uprightly."—Psalm lxxxiv. 11.

I felt I did not love Thee, Lord!
E'en as I should, just as I ought;
The vain delights earth's joys afford,
My erring fitful soul had caught.

So bent I low before Thy throne,
That Thou might'st draw me nearer Thee,
And, with the blood of Thy dear Son,
From sin's deep stains might'st set me free.

What would I more, if Thou would'st make
My feet to walk at Thy command,
And on towards heaven's high portal take
And gently lead me by the hand?

Yet still this wayward, earth-bound soul
Would sigh for worldly treasures vain;
I did not dare to tell the whole,
Nor ask for all I sighed to gain.

But Thou, who know'st my inmost heart,
And all 'twere vain to hide from Thee—
So great a God of love thou art—
More than I asked Thou grantedst me!

Thou gav'st me treasures far more rare
Than all earth's fleeting wealth can buy;
And placedst me in Thy Spirit's care,
To train me for Thy child on high.

What would I more? And yet 'twas Thou
That this life's blessings round me spread,
With beams of health lit up my brow,
And in sweet spots my footsteps led.

Yea, e'en the secret wish I nurst,
Thou didst not even that deny!
And Thou who gav'st me pardon first,
Gav'st every other rich supply.

Grant, Lord! that nothing Thou hast given
Of earthly gifts, so soon to flee,
May ever stay my course to heaven,
Or tear my foolish heart from Thee.

Thou gavest more than I desired,
More than I ever could deserve;
Oh, be my heart by Thee inspired,
Thee first, Thee only here to serve.

And be each sinful thing removed,
Each idol that has filled my breast,
That Thou be, undivided, loved,
And I in Thee alone be blest.

Cleansed from each guilty thought—forgiven—
A heart renewed by Thee I crave;
My prayer—that I be trained for heaven—
'Tis more than I deserve to have.

The Church,

SEE COLLECT FOR SIXTEENTH SUNDAY AFTER TRINITY.

The streamlet, from the fountain shining,
Runs at the foot of the gentle hill;
At the end of the mead, like a silvery lining,
'Tis running and sparkling still:
So our Holy Catholic Church, from its Head,
Tho' small, ran pure and clean,
And through the dark world on, on it sped,
Far glimmered its silvery sheen.

And the parched-up land hath drunk and revived,
It hath tasted the cooling spring;
And the drooping flow'ret hath sipped and lived,
And the wild, waste places sing!

And the heathen shores have stol'n down to the stream
That hath opened its welcoming flood;
And the darkness is scared by the gentle gleam,
And the pagan bends low before God!

The streamlet, no longer a tiny rill,
But a river bounding and wide,
Hath passed on from the haunt of its childhood still,
By the quiet mountain side;
Thro' the noisy city's revel and roar
Its far-spreading waters flow;
But that which was shining and clear before,
Is polluted and blackened now.

The Church so pure in its earlier days,
When a little but resolute throng;
That had flowed on thro' rough and thro' rugged ways,
In its very weakness strong—
Hath courted the world's vast multitude,
In the cities and haunts of men;
But with error's dark stream it became imbued,
And it lost its first lustre then.

Full many a time (as His people of old)
Might its Lord have renounced it quite;
But strong was His love for His erring fold,
Tho' no longer pure and white;
And we read of its numberless perils past,
Of its errors and follies forgiven,

And we know He will guide it to the last,
Till it flows in the ocean of heaven.

O Lord! Thou hast looked on Thy Church's ways,
How far it hath wandered from Thee;
Oh, recal not the sins of its former days!
Restore it, and set it free
To the men of the world a reproach it is now,
And its sons have caused its shame;
Oh, cleanse it, and cause it once more to flow
As when clear from the fountain it came!

MUSINGS AMONG THE MOUNTAINS,

The mountains stand round about, and their very silence is perpetual praise.

Their rugged sternness displays His majesty, and their verdant carpet His goodness.

They spread forth their lesser green slopes and gentler undulations to the valleys; so hath He respect unto the simple, and condescends to send forth His ambassadors to treat with the children of men.

The moss that is trodden on, is the carpet of the high rock; so many that suffer earth's contumely are the nearest to heaven.

The lowly sheep feed on the mountain summit; so humility is true exaltation.

They go down into the thronged plains and are sacrificed for men; so did He come down from his high dwelling-place to be sacrificed for us.

As the sheep of the mountain come down to be a sacrifice for man, so in descending to daily self-sacrifice are we most preparing ourselves for the mountain summit of the everlasting land.

The thick clouds oftentimes rest on the high mountain; so also trouble must be passed through on our way to the gates of heaven.

The peaks of the high hills catch the latest sunrays; so in silent and lofty contemplation may we find most of heaven.

MISCELLANEOUS POEMS.

SECTION II.

THE SUNNY SIDE.

"Let the dead past bury its dead."—LONGFELLOW.

I WOULD have sung in more enlivening strain,
Clearer, and less depressing; for we minstrels
Seem all infected by the same dull breathings—
Though some in nobler song and others meaner;
We all weep o'er our empty caskets, vases
Broken, their faded flowers all strewn around,
Dead joys, and rainbow hopes, and palling pleasures,
And vain desires, and blighted prospects, and
The sunny spring of youth chilled into winter!
So in mysterious moanings of a something
Shadowy and ill-defined, yet wrapt around us,
We go, all listless, musing, dreaming on,
'Midst thorns that wound us, culling pleasure-flowers;
So we go warbling forth our plaintive harpings,
Half wild, half sweet, yet melancholy ever;
So are we saddening others, and ourselves
Lashing with flails of ills half conjured up;—
Just as to-morrow's racer starves himself

To win the laurelled wreath—for poesy's crown
We feed on fancied griefs, and see a blight
On every ear of hope that waves to-day;
And so the unfolded aspect of our life
(At least the life we picture to the world)
Is one vast grave-yard where the dead past lies,
Lit by cold moonlight rays of sad remembrance,
Where the night-breaths of buried hopes brush by,
And sweep our heart-chords with æolian touches,
Half wild, half sweet, but melancholy ever;
Where phantom joys flit past, and ghosts of days
That Time long since wrapped in their winding
 sheets,
Start up before us on their cold tombs lying;
And spectre shades of coming sorrow haunt us,
For we sap up the healthy dews strewn round us,
That shining speak to us of blithesome morn,
In gentle whisperings breathing patience; heedless,
We lay our widowed hearts upon the pyre,
And all life's future rises in a mist
Of dull raw doubtings, and a dusky mantle
Of unbelief, that reds the cheerful sunrise,
Or veils it altogether. Like the child's game,
Where light of simple Truth spreads all around,
We love to blind our eyes, and grope in darkness!
As if we thought to make its nearness distant
(Using the wrong end of the instrument),
So we might prate about fictitious strivings
In self-made mists, so glorying when we grasp it.
And so our tired peruser, much preferring

The cheerful fact to lonely chilling fancies,
Closes the volume, shaking off the night-mare
In the unhaunted day-fact of real life;
And solaces himself, content and happy,
In round of business, or on couch of pleasure;
And thus is poesy banished as a scarecrow.

I would have sung a more enlivening strain
Of brightening fires of friendship and affection,
Heaped up with fuel of a cherished past,
Glowing all down the long dim corridor
Of life's unravelled future, kindling gloom
At least with mantling ray of happiness;
Thus had I sung—but oh, how can I sing
Strain that shall falsify or contrast theirs?
Am I more favoured? Have I then no hope
Green once, sered now? no jewelled treasure stolen?
No fondest idol doted on, crushed, crumbled?
Have I no grave-yard of the past to mourn in?
No fond delight, slow-worked, but soon unthreaded?
I cannot, may not still my heart's low whisper,
That will add its share to earth's load of trouble;
For, like the seven hues nature weaves together
And fashions them into her arch of light,
A ripening bliss reared, cherished, nursed, nay, more!
All wov'n into my life—but not a seventh,
For then had six parts yet remained to me;
But what seemed well nigh all, nor knew of bounds—
Wrought in, too soon to be expelled again!

From her young love I filled my soul with bliss—
But sudden torn from old association,
Replanted in all new and stranger bowers,
Time snatched up quick the cup my heart desired,
Spilt its contents, refilled it with fresh liquid,
And though I loathed, stood by, and made me drink it,
And in his later sweets renounce the old ones,
And vainly strive to sip the emptied sweets,
So charmed and glutted with the newer nectar,
Made a base traitor to my own prized feelings,
A traitor 'spite myself, 'spite all my yearnings
To feel again the joys I prized of yore!
But oh! a truce to these all-saddening feelings;
I would have sung a livelier, better strain;
I would have—why not? Why should I forbear?
Come out, and close the gates where dead regrets
Lie buried in their lonesome cemetery;
Come on life's present busy bustling plain,
Where active duties swarm, a genial throng!
Methinks no spectre-grief can haunt me there.
Come with me, O glad muse of sprightly teaching!
Tune me to sing of gay activity,
Of woe chased off by active cheerfulness,
Of doubt dispelled by living Christian faith!

Go, join that pleasant throng beside the hearth;
With merry converse tell the daily gossip,
Of social sweets and harmless pleasure chatting,
Fill up the gap of time till duty call thee,

Or slumber soft and sweet with painless visions
Prepare thee for the day of energy.
Let Maiden Morn array thee armour proof,
Strong in thyself and fit to fight for others;
See that o'er this she throw her shining robe,
Her gladdening garb of active cheerfulness.
Equipped—no more alone, but 'mid thy fellows—
Stand in strong phalanx, fearless of the foe;
Stand, but go not to rush upon their lines;
They will attack too soon; just wait for them;
To-morrow's might may bear to-morrow's strife.
Hide thine own sorrow in thy breast, and go
Relieve the poor, and soothe the sorrowing ones,
And whisper words of comfort to the afflicted;
Shed rays of hope on each despairing one,
Share others' griefs, and thine own happy moments
Let others share with thee; come joy or sorrow,
Pass through them, acting, living in the present,
But living for a sure undimmed hereafter.
And when thou next shalt feel thy griefs, so lessened
And dwindled they shall be, thou scarce shalt know them.
Be like a ship; upon the waves of life
Ride fearless, cut the black and foaming billows;
Ride on, and soon thou'lt pass the frowning confines,
With thy lamp lit, a beacon be to others!
For if, like pilot ship to rescue wreck'd ones,
The boiling surges toss thee on their breasts,

When thou hast hailed, hast saved thy drowning
comrades,
Thy joy shall calm for thee the angry waters;
Thou shalt forget thou too hast shared the tempest.
Ride on, and when in soft and sunny fairways,
Sip the sweet calm, but still sail on nor linger!
Let not the coy wind woo thee into waiting;
Ride on, tho' soon another storm enshroud thee;
For through thy glass — that glass which every
mariner
On life's drear main may have, if he'll but use it—
Clear and more plain the city-walls of jasper,
Its pier of precious stones, the stormless waters,
Where heaven's unclouded Sun of Righteousness
Silvers the rippling flood with sacred splendour!
That is thy haven; ride on, then, all fearless,
Braving the storm-wind — scorning too to linger
In that calm spot encircled with the tempest—
Ride on, and enter the celestial harbor,
And anchor near the shores of perfect peace,
And unalloyed, eternal happiness!

I have no doubtings of the coming future;
I know it, if be mine that present now
That I would sing of, useful and ennobling,
That shuns a dead past, scorns a dulled hereafter,
But points and beckons to a clear, unclouded,
All real, eternal, fixed reality.
This be my song-theme. Poet who reign'st to-
day!

Had I thy vigor, and one half thy beauty!
Oh, when thou hast sealed up thy deathless verse,
Give me thy mantle, teach me how to wear it!
Be mine the theme—no dull despairing one—
But thine the deep and vigorous inspiration!

SPRING'S APPROACH.

THE days are growing longer now,
The sun is coming back;
Clearer we view that steep hill's brow
Rise in that rural track.
And Winter's gloom shall soon depart,
Spring bound o'er hill and plain;
But Winter yet reigns in my heart,
Nor Spring returns again!

The cold white snow shall melt away,
The ice-framed gems shall fade;
And Winter shall renounce his sway
Beneath the tall trees' shade.
In fresh-clad bloom each flower shall start,
Where drops the genial rain;
But Winter quits not yet my heart,
Nor Spring returns again!

And Spring's soft balm shall warm the gale,
Shall fill Eve's pearly dew;
And Spring's sweet flowers shall grace the vale
With tints of richest hue.
O for the balm within my heart
To melt the icy chain,
That Winter might indeed depart,
And it be Spring again!

Ruler of nature! at Whose voice
The seasons come and go,
Who bid'st us in glad Spring rejoice,
And with fresh rapture glow:
The sunshine of Thy grace impart—
Oh melt the icy chain!
Chase the dark Winter from my heart,
And give me Spring again.

OVERSANDS.

AN ALLEGORY.

"Across the sands, the yellow sands!
Bright sparkling 'neath the noonday sun—
The shortest track to yon bright lands,
An easier journey, sooner done.
Oh, 'tis a fair and pleasant way!
Gay gleaming far beneath your feet
The blue-lit waters of the bay,
Calm with slow rippling tread, retreat.
No rough or craggy hill to ascend,
Or clamber up yon toilsome steep;
On one smooth plain the way to wend,
Along that level tract to keep;
To rest beneath the tall cliff's shade,
And gather sea-shells glittering low ——"
"Enough is said; the choice is made:
Such charms to allure!—that way I go."

When Pharaoh's war-clad chariots sped
In hot pursuit their prey to take,
Along that sea-retreating bed,
Though swift their perilled way they make—
Too late to turn and flee away,
Too soon to reach the longed-for goal—
Upon that helpless, hopeless prey
Back, back the threatening waters roll!

So the charmed traveller rambles on,
Along that open level way;
The soft smooth yellow sands upon,
Secure his eager footsteps stray.
Afar the calm blue ocean lies,
Whose rippling music charms his ear;
Beyond those distant cliffs arise—
He little dreams of danger near!

But changed the scene! the breeze runs wild,
And heavy threatening storm-clouds rear
Their lurid shapes, in masses piled
Above the waters, dark and drear!
With muttering thunders on they come,
Borne by the fast increasing gale;
Proud stalking o'er each crest of foam,
Where renten rides the distant sail.
Down, down the cliffs the torrents pour,
In eddying floods along the sand;
With louder and yet louder roar
The billows climb the sloping strand;
The tide has turned! and softer now
That soft smooth sand, beneath the tread
Of that despairing one, sunk low,
As on with wilder haste he sped.
But vain his speed—that mocking coast
Will from his anxious eyes retreat;
That pathway, late his joy and boast,
Sinks lower yet beneath his feet.

So bright, and yet so smooth and dry,
At morn those glittering quicksands lay,
When the glad sunshine lit the sky,
And ocean rolled awhile away.
But, 'neath night's shade engulphed and lost,
That fated traveller—where was he,
While the wild sea-foam lashed the coast,
And billowing specked the angry sea?
Go, ask those glad ones on the shore:
No stranger to their bright realms came;
'Tis but the lonely sea-wave's roar
Shall wailing sound that lost one's name.

O traitorous yellow sands of earth!
So fair, so firm awhile that seem,
By men esteemed of so much worth,
While suns of gladness o'er them gleam!
But let the waves of trouble rise,
And let the floods of sorrow fall,
And that same wealth that men so prize,
Say, shall it then avail at all?
Vain hope, to reach the heavenly gates
On earthly gold thy easy way!
The same sad fate thy steps awaits,
And death's dark flood engulphs its prey.
The paths of duty must thou keep,
The tall cliff's side, the thorny road;
The rougher track across the steep,
That only leads to heaven and God.

But weary art thou, weak and sore?
And fearful shrinks thy fainting soul?
There's One has trod these paths before;
'Tis He shall guide thee to the goal.

OLD FRIENDS.

Where are the friends I prized of yore—
Bright circlet of my youthful days?
All scattered now! and I no more
Beside them tread those pleasant ways.

Bright circlet! yea, for one dear gem
Among that group conspicuous shone;
And for her sake I think of them,
And would remember every one.

Some grow estranged and keep away,
And others cross the trackless sea;
New faces crowd life's stage to-day;
And but their names are left to me.

So, like the apparel of the ball,
Bright though youth's glittering diadem be,
All fancy's fleeting gems soon fall,
And leave the world's bare truth to me.

Yet would I fain that cluster wear
In memory still my heart beside;
At least let that one gem be there,
Though all its lustre long since died.

Gleam on awhile, youth's sunset ray!
Her image on my soul I'll see;
And I'll recall those friends to-day,
Whom Time's chill stream hath swept from me.

THE RESERVOIR.

AN ALLEGORY.

A spacious reservoir, embanked, flashed forth
In sheet of light that glazed its liquid carpet;
Stores of clear water from Artesian springs
Welled up to gleam 'neath Nature's teeming dome,
Ere long to lace the meads with silver linings.
Not yet disturb it; let it rest untouched,
Till there be formed complete its channelled way.
Not yet, or else, in maddening fury falling,
'Twill flush the fields, scare off the tinted green,
And sweep along in one unbounded flood
To the great ocean, useless and dishonored,
Brief as a stream of light that streaks the sky.

Would'st thou the flood-gates now unbar? Too soon!
Remember, I have warned thee of thy folly;
Thou canst not close again the unbarred exit,
Nor stay the all-resistless force let loose.
"Ah! see the shining floods, how well they glide!
We can patch up a channel where unfinished."
Prepare to see thy poor endeavours useless.
'Tis done! they overflow. Oh, dire confusion!
Oh, flood all unresisted! Close the gates!
Alas! they were not framed to close again.
See how they pour down, down upon the lowlands!
See how they pour; bring all your powers to stay
them;
Rear artificial barriers, rear them up!
'Twere vain; thou canst not stay the moving mass,
Or check the onward impetus once given.
It will, methinks, have vent, will flow out somewhere;
And when arrives the time it most is needed,
Oh, will not well-nigh all have 'scaped for ever,
Wasted, misspent, let loose in untrue channels—
Wasted, misspent, the reservoir all emptied?
"But what," say you, "is that to thee or me?"
O man, 'tis well indeed if it be nothing!
But you and I, can we both stand acquitted?
Say, are there no rich reservoirs of love,
No treasured springs, that were designed for blessings
A bounteous Heaven rained down for righteous usings
In their due time in one appointed channel,
That thou hast changed by thine own vain devisings,
Impatient graspings, unprepared receivings—
Changed into curses? Gifts misspent and wasted,

Gifts that for good to thee to employ were given?
"But what speaks this of that to thee or me?"
Nay, man! I need not turn interpreter;
There is the picture, go and read its meaning—
There the corn lies, be thine own conscience gleaner—
Ask thine own heart, I will not answer thee.

WATCHING FOR THE CHANGE.

When will the weather break? Wind of the west,
Zephyr of spring-time, come, come o'er the main!
Come, for we love thy warm wooings the best;
Scare back the snow-blast, break winter's cold chain!

Come, for the east wind is reigning below;
Come, for the sun-warmth waits trembling on high,
Fearing to face the cold front of the foe—
Come to the rescue, sweet queen of the sky!

April is ended, and glad May is here;
Yet dost thou linger—why, why so unkind?
Nature is weeping, she waits thee to cheer;
Loth dost thou leave thy soft south land behind?

Come, ere the hope of our heart wane away;
Come, ere the life we have loved so have fled.
Lord of creation! to Thee do we pray;
Roll back the blast, send the zephyr instead!

One hope remains yet—if but the chill wind,
Sated, retire to his polar domain,
Ere the frail flow'ret too firmly he bind,
Spring may then loose, may revive her again.

Close fast the window; keep out the cold breath—
Oh for the balm of the summer again!
Weaker and paler—oh! wilt thou not, Death,
Wait thee one moment? Poor hope! thou art vain.

Gentle spring-zephyr! we hail thee at last!
Why didst thou linger till death seized his prey?
Now thou art with us, when hope is all past,
Come but to waft the freed spirit away.

Burst forth in beauty, ye buds in your bowers!
Flow forth afresh in the gleam, gentle rill!
Wave ye, green leaves, wet with spring's balmy
showers!
Healer of nature! my fainting heart fill!

CENTRED HOPES.

On what a fragile cord earth's joys are fixed!
Our hopes are like the rays of streaming light
That spread athwart our world from out the spheres;
And as on Time's swift wing we wend our way
To the one centre, to the point itself—
That star of time, that focus of our wishes,
The day, the hour desired so eagerly—
Oh! what a little, what a trifling cause
May snap in twain hope's shallow stream of light!

Could ye but reach yon stars that blaze so brightly,
Might ye not lose the lustre that ye love
In vast unbrightened realms of rigid fact,
Bare mountain-regions of eternal snows?
So reach we oft the summit of our hopes,
To find their centred points grey, cold, and dull;
Or some, perchance, may prove mere meteor-gleams,
Whose centres as we near them glide away,
Or vanish into visioned nothingness.

Thus bask our souls upon these beams of bliss;
Thus from their far-off focus draw we down
The unsubstantial food they feed upon.
And so when hope's gay gleam breaks suddenly,

When meteor-joys unreal glide away,
How empty seem we! how unnerved, unfit
To cope with disappointment! easy preys
Our lean unnourished hearts too soon become.

There's many a fair oäsis in life's wastes
That time shall waft our wearied souls upon;
And well indeed it were to wait them calmly,
Enjoy them with hearts fraught with thankfulness.
But oh! those sweet yet wearying streams of hope,
That stretch our weak, frail hearts to distant specks,
Dim in the future, yet so fondly cherished—
Those longed for, anxiously-awaited epochs
That, after all, perchance may never come,
Or coming, prove scarce worth the waiting for!
If sinless pleasures rightly were received,
Yet never longed for with intense desires,
If reaching quick-receding realms of joy,
On one star higher still our gaze were fixed—
One polar light, alone unchangeable,
The one true sun, the sure unswerving point
Round which all earth and heaven shall ceaseless roll,
Where links of pure delight alone are forged,
And joy's real fires undying ever burn,
In Him who is the one great Fount of good,
The only author of true happiness—

ıen should we calmly use earth's present pleasures;
'hile our grand hope, our future longing then
'ould be the mirth sin's moth can ne'er corrupt,
ıat sterling joy that disappointeth not.

YOU AND I.

I WOULD inscribe for thee a lay;
But young Love's muse seems silent now,
Fled with the past her strains away:
And I, alas! no more know how.

All vain I strive to pen the line,
Meet offering for a maiden fair—
A richer tribute should be thine
Than this sered heart could now prepare.

So when I seek my thoughts to write,
The words come feebly, weak and slow;
As if my heart had winged its flight
To bask beneath that dead past's glow.

But if, that volumed store to fill,
Too little else, be left for thee,
Take all I have, for *her* sake still—
Be (if no more) a friend to me.

Near in our summer-time of bliss,
So mingled with that joy of yore,
I could not view you less than this,
A cherished friend, if nothing more.

Kindred of hers! enough, methinks,
Were this to weave a closer tie,
And (if no more) with friendship's links
At least, to bind us, you and I.

These be my promptings; would 'twere thine
To be henceforth my future light!
In thee the dim past cease to shine,
Thy gay beams sunning sorrow's night!

There; now I cease—love's errant muse,
Awhile recalled, is hastening by—
How shall it be? Say; you must choose—
Friends, then (if no more), you and I?

ON THE BRIDGE.

STANDING on the crowded bridge,
  Where the thousands come and go,
Watched I then that far-off ridge,
  Calm above the river's flow.
Summer-time and summer-balm
  Floated o'er me, and I wove
Round that hill-top such sweet charm,
  Cherished hopes of changeless love.
Verdant throne of rural peace!
  'Mid the circling tumult, still!
Brimmed my heart with blissful ease,
  While I watched that distant hill.

But the summer zephyrs flee,
  And the winter rude blasts roar,
And the mists have veiled from me
  That green hill I viewed before.
Passed unto his southern track,
  Lo! the sun grows weak and chill;
But ere long he shall come back,
  Burning, beam above the hill.

Winter on the icy blast—
  Winter in the chilly air—
Winter round my soul has cast
  Its ice-chain, and fastened there!

To the zephyrs from the sea
  Leaps each freed and flashing rill;
Mid the clearer air I see
  See once more the distant hill:
Standing on the crowded bridge,
  While the myriads come and go,
View again its verdant ridge,
  Where the widening waters flow.
But the mists lie on my soul;
  Veiled those cherished charms of yore!
And that winter-mist shall roll
  Off my heart, oh! nevermore.

LOVE AND PRIDE.

AN ALLEGORY.

In the heaven of heavens, around the throne of the Eternal One, the highest and brightest of the angel-throng were weeping over the fall and degradation of the sons of men, the deprivation of their happiness, and the loss of their earthly Paradise. Then one of the chief among those shining beings volunteered to go forth as a messenger of consolation, and solicited a few drops of the celestial essence, that it might, by its divine instilling, preserve the fallen world from becoming altogether a hell. And her Almighty Sovereign graciously permitted her to fulfil her desire; and He said unto her "Go;" and she went forth, and her mission and her title was Love. And so amid the many endearments of life—between mother and child, friend and friend, husband and wife—there was yet a something found which rendered earth not so irretrievably wretched after all; for the Angel-messenger worked on very silently and surely there.

But there was rage and dire vexation at the court *of the Arch Fiend*; and summoned were his hellish councillors, to debate how they might best counteract the good influence that had marred their miserable triumph, and flecked the gloom of their earthly abiding-place with sunshine:

"Where match we the meddling power that has dared to interfere with our kingdom, and to thwart its complete subjugation—crevicing the dungeon of despair, and causing a ray of heaven's own light to peer through?"

So they sent Sensuality; and the tall tares grew up boldly and defiantly among Love's slender wheat-ears. Touch them not! Let them both grow up together to the harvest.

Meanwhile the Angel-messenger, ever desirous of unity, and ever working for harmonious peace, trailed the wild weed-plant, and grafted it on the purer stalk, to check its uncurbed blossomings, and to temper its bold luxuriance; and there sprang up from that union a plant at least good enough for the earthly soil of its cultivation; watered anon by her tears, and sunned by her smiles.

And the rage of the foiled fiends burst forth afresh in fiercer fury; and they sought for yet another, powerful enough to undo the work. Then stalked forth one out of that ghostly throng, and he seemed the mightiest and most malignant of them all.

"I will go forth," he said, "and I will become an idol, enthroned and cherished in the hearts of men; and I will mingle with Love's flourishing plants, and spread, locust-like, over her cultivated fields; and I will be a blight on the buddings of affection, and will wither them, that they die, and yield no fruit."

And the Arch Fiend bade him go, and the whole army of hell hissed out in their triumphant spleen. And he went forth, and his name and his nature was Pride.

Then there arose fresh warfare upon earth; and from that time forth man warred against himself, and became his own enemy. Then began he, too, to immolate himself, and not even as the pagan for a future unrevealed, but for a brief present span of heroic misery, to cast his own heart on the pyre, for the honour and glory of the monster-god; and from age to age the kind word remained unuttered, and the little explanation deferred; and hearts lay writhing, gloomed in their self-reared prison-house, and galled by their own forged chains; and kin and kin, family and family, the parent and the child, the husband and the wife, and the lover and the beloved one, kept apart, and buried their irrepressible yearnings in the chill o'erflowings of their unsullied dignity, and the petty consolation of their uncompromising pride; and few were the corn-ears that were pure and blighted not.

For the only course now open to true affection (and herein is the lesson to be learnt and the object gained), is in self-humiliation; and the first germs of unkind *feeling* must be eradicated by mutual explanation sought for and rendered, even though we lower ourselves thereby; for only he who is daily lowering himself in the estimation of his own proud nature shall exalt himself in the realizing that truer happiness which Love holds in store for him. So shall petty misunderstandings vanish, and the seedlings of a great wrong be trampled down in their birth; for as it is true of heaven itself, so also of heaven's own Love: there is no path thereto but by the crosses of self-abasement and self-humiliation.

So only shall our hearts' love grow up, sweetly cherished by the Messenger Angel's care; so only shall it become meet for those celestial garners, where alike the coarser grains of Sensuality and the festering blights of Pride may never enter to mar that richer fruitfulness garnered for Love's pure and inexhaustible treasury, 'mid the ever-ripening harvest-fields of heaven.

PROLOGUE

TO AN AMATEUR PERFORMANCE OF "BROKEN TOYS."

WHEN from afar resounds the increasing roar,
As the turned tide-waves climb the shelving shore,
And snow-foamed billows, in tumultuous moan,
Lash the red sand, and make its spoils their own,
And sweeping on in their resistless force,
Whelm in relentless flood the opposers of their course;
Yet on the sands the merry children play,
Nor heed the boiling surge, the blinding spray;
Play on, all safe beneath the sunbeam's glow,
All fearless of the floods that rage below;
And when dark tempest-cloud has veiled the sky,
Secure retreat they to their dwellings nigh.

So we—while war's dread seas have ebbed away,
And left the nations lulled in peace to-day—
Catch, 'mid the calm, the moaning of the main,
As if its red waves rolled them back again,
Ere long to lash the lands with fiercer flood,
Stain smiling scenes with crimsoned tide of blood.
So we, too, like the merry children, play
Safe on the shore, in cheerful converse gay;
Nor fear the advancing floods; for well we know
There are glad spots its billows ne'er o'erflow;

There are high lands its waves may never reach—
Just like the children, safe upon the beach!
Just like the traveller, 'neath the o'er-arching dome,
Alike from storm-cloud safe and ocean foam!
Sweet scene secure! where may war never come!
That spot is here—is in our English home.

Here, then, we greet you—though dread rumor falls,
And all without with hovering gloom appals—
Here peaceful sit awhile, within these walls,
And we will strive, obedient to your calls,
Our little play before you to perform;
Your smiles shall be to us the sunbeams warm,
Your disapproval our (far-distant) storm!
We feel you will not be too harsh to-night,
But view our failings in a kindlier light;
And we will do our best to amuse and please,
Assured we play beside all smiling seas.

You who love mirth—would revel in her ray—
May find, we trust, a little in our play;
Ye sentimental ones who'd woo her gale,
Along her varying tears and smiles would sail—
Whilst on the current of our play you ride,
Weep when you please, but give some smiles beside.
There lurks a fragrance in each fleeting hour,
E'en tho' its shape be gaudy pleasure-flower;
We may sip sweets in mirth's more sterile way,
Gain something good when we are light and gay;
Though violet-hours 'neath holier shades but lie,
Sure pleasure's sunny sward is graced the daisy by!

You'll hear to-night of fickle Fortune's pranks;
How she her votaries leads along her ranks;
Now 'mid rich bowers of golden wealth they stroll,
Now on adversity's drear waters roll;
Now, the storm weathered, landing in the cove
Of gentle peace, experience knit to love!
You'll hear how honest avocations bless,
And humble trades reap rich and sure success;
While some "genteel" profession soon may be,
In idle hands, the path of penury.
How love (but that's of course by no means new)
Points, like the compass, in all weathers true.
But chief, and this the moral of our play
(And I'll with this conclude, and go my way):
Hide thine own griefs within thine aching breast;
With smiles cheer others, so shalt thou be blest.
In harmless mirth and genial cheerfulness
Bathe well thy heart-wounds; they will pain thee less;
In Christian duties work the livelong day,
But fill the gaps with sinless pleasure's ray;
Illumined thus, thy griefs shall melt away.
So mourn no more thy time-departed joys,
So cease to idly weep o'er thy heart's "Broken Toys."

A NEW YEAR'S GIFT.

"Let it alone this year also."—Luke xiii. 8.

"How shall He not with Him also freely give us all things?"—
Rom. viii. 32.

Let him alone! Keep off thy heavy hand,
Nor crush that spirit-tenement of clay,
Imaged so fair, and yet so frail and weak!
Off, fell disease! and do thy work elsewhere.
And thou, O child of man! listen to me,
And I will tell thee, at this infant epoch,
This first glad hour of mine appointed year,
The gifts I am prepared to bless thee with.

I send my angel, Health, to thee from heaven,
Laden with holy sweets and saving ointment
Of vigor and of elasticity.
She shall anoint thy limbs with precious oil,
Shall fill thy feeble frame and fainting heart
With healing balm of hope and buoyancy;
Thy spirits, no more ebbing, clogged, and low,
In freshened flow shall fill their channelled way;
Yea, they shall pour from out thy beaming eyes,
And tinge thy tinted cheek with ruddier glow.
O man! this is my New Year's Gift to thee:
Say, shall I bear no tribute back again?

Yet more: I give thee dear delights of home,
And all the charms that social converse yields;
I place thy feet in friendship's pleasant paths;
I give thee honest hearts to glad thine own,
Bright faces, gentle forms, to smile on thee,
The sun of cheerfulness to light thy way,
Affection's glow to warm thy kindling soul.
This is the New Year's Gift I bring to thee:
What pledge of gratitude wilt thou return?

For thee the fruitful fields, and verdant vales,
The snow-peaked mountain, and the high hill-top,
Shall laugh and joy beneath another spring;
And zephyr-wings shall fan the parching air,
When the high summer sun resplendent burns,
Ripening rich stores I treasure up for thee,
Prepared in Autumn's golden granary.
And thou art free to wander forth, unfettered,
To revel in the rich delights of nature;
Her cooling breath shall be upon thy brow,
Thy feet shall move in swifter, nimbler tread.
This is my New Year's Gift. What, silent yet!
Hast thou no word, no look of love for me?

Yet stay; thou hast offended grievously,
And thou dost wrong me still each passing day—
Here is thy pardon; oft it has been proffered;
Again I tender it; 'twas purchased with
The holy life and precious cleansing blood
Of *my own holy*, well-beloved Son.

'Twill claim, besides those gifts I now have named,
A future title, heirship, right of entrance
To my eternal, wholly happy home,
Whose joys, too great for even utterance here,
Thou may'st not know now, but thou shalt hereafter.

Thus have I come at midnight's solemn hour,
While sounds the death-knell of the closing year,
When I receive its living register,
Its filled-up record of the written past—
Thus have I come, and stand before thy soul,
With countless gifts to grace thy glad New Year.
I know not what beside I could have offered—
If thou desirest more, but ask, and have.

And now I re-ascend to Heaven's high altar;
The holy salver there must be replaced;
Shall no thank-offering fill the sacred bowl,
No incense of a grateful, loving heart
Ascend with me to those eternal courts,
In joyful tribute of adoring praise?

These are my gifts, O child of earth! to thee.
I wish thee ——— nay, I *give* my glad New Year!
What is thine answer? How respondest thou?
What dost thou say, O man? what give to me?

WINTER.

A SKETCH.

The summer balmy hours had flown,
And winter chilled the air;
And she sat in that silent room alone—
A maiden young and fair;
And the wintry wind, with its dying moan,
Was her sole companion there.

Too weak to face the cold blast now,
To seek new joys elsewhere;
For the tints of health were stealing slow
From that face so young and fair;
And she thought of the spring-time's sunny glow,
And of him, no longer there!

She had won his heart in early spring,
When eve's soft dews shone clear;
But she deemed it some mere trifling thing
(Love's costliest treasure dear!);
So she spurned it, soon to take new wing
In *that winter* lone and drear—

To roam away to each gladsome place
Where health and beauty reign,
Where sincere is the smile on each youthful face;
To roam—but no longer in vain;
In the truthful glance of some bright eyes trace
How love can be loved again.—

But why so muse on the past, and on him
Who has ceased to be aught to her?
Why should such thoughts in the twilight dim
Her heaving bosom stir?
She will not think any longer of him
Who was nothing—no, nothing to her!

She will not whisper that once-loved name,
Whose love she forbade to flow;
Or yearn for the heart she had scorned to claim—
She needed no lover now!
Though he might have supported that sinking frame,
And have soothed her aching brow.

But the absent tones of that slighted one
Still seemed to fill her ear,
E'en as in the sunny summer gone,
When the days were long and clear;
She heard it above the dull winds moan,
In that winter twilight drear.

Perchance she regretted her self-willed fate
That had spurned him from her side;

Perchance she repented her scorn and hate,
And her unforgiving pride.
But the rough blast wailed forth "Too late!" "Too late!"
The chilling night-wind sighed.

While the waning moon with its mistiest beams
Pierces, wan thro' the rifted cloud,
Upon yon white wall too soon it seems
To have woven her white cold shroud!
Oh, why all lone 'mid such startling dreams,
While her heart beats fast and loud?

It may be she wished him with her now,
To comfort her and to cheer,
While the ebbing tide of life ran low,
And earth's last hours seemed near.
It may be, while winter storm blasts blow,
She sheds one sorrowing tear—
Enough; forgive her, and leave her so:
There is retribution here.

TIME.

I SAW him pass! Magician mightier
Than Egypt's mightiest—earth's great sorcerer—
The undying wizard—despot undethroned!
Rearing, and ruling, altering, withering all things;
Forcing reluctant but enfeebled mortals
To do his bidding, to obey his nod.
Come we and track his footsteps, mark his wonders—
Master of mind, as well as lord of matter—
All unresisted conqueror, tyrant Time!

He came to the poor peasant's cot.—The boy
Who stood beside the wood-log on the hearth,
Had just returned from labor at the plough,
With hob-nailed shoes and rough cord jacket clad—
Soiled hands and face — yet on whose dark brow reigned
Deep thought, and fixed her visioned palace there.
His mother busy spread the scanty meal—
Perchance coarse oaten bread and water-porridge—
His father rested on the hard wood-chair;
While thriving artizans erect passed by,
And thanked their stars that that was not their home.
But Time came there, and looked upon the lad,

And spake in tone of calm complacency :
"Poor boy! but thou shalt in thy peasant-cot
Become a beacon, for a future age
To gaze upon with rapture. I will fan
The mists of chilling penury; they shall glow
Around thee, like a halo fresh from heaven;
And all the great ones of the busy world
Shall join to reverence the peasant-boy."
But the boy stands in dreamy wonderment;
The father gazes with derisive scorn;
The mother half in hope, half unbelief.
Yet Time he knew his story to be true;
And so it proved. "But," say ye, "he had that,
His spring of honor, which Time cannot give,
The spark 'tis his to fan into the flame
That thrilled the enlightened world with ecstasy."
Well, be it so; yet could not he have quenched it?
"Nay!" say a hundred voices, "nay, not so!
The spark of genius never pales nor dies;
It flashes forth to ages yet unborn."
Aye, that is true; but may the fire blaze still,
When its first shrine a heap of embers lies?
So shall the shrine of deathless genius be;
All dark and broken, crumbled into dust,
Shrouded in gloom. So yet, methinks, 'tis true,
Time does extinguish that he never gave:
There's but one spark death's waters cannot dim.

But lo! we pause, and Time is beckoning us;
Come, let us on.

Some ragged urchin, tired,
Shoeless, and penniless, that begged his way
From the mean hamlet in his native village,
To the proud halls where Commerce holds her court,
And thronging multitudes bend low before her,
With them to crawl and fawn before her footstool—
Time comes to him, and breathes a yellow breath,
And henceforth all he touches turns to gold,
And London streets to him seem paved with wealth;
Whate'er he grasps is tenfold multiplied.
And now, exalted to the right-hand seat,
Erect and proud he sits beside the queen,
Where once he crouched; and flattering sycophants
Extol the man—"the mighty man of wealth,"
"Patron of commerce," "of immense estate!"
And he, he feels and owns himself a king,
And looks on wealth as all his natural right,
As if with master-mind he'd gotten it.
But Time moves on, nor heeds his ingrate child—
Smiles with contempt, for well he knows too soon
He can reclaim his unacknowledged treasure,
And give it unto others.
So passing on,
Far greater wizard he than they of old—
The fairies that now charm earth's soil no more,
All buried in traditions of the past—
So passing on, Change, his prime minister,
Hastens his every nod with speed to obey;
And with a touch of his most magic wand,
The poor, the mean, the outcast of the earth

Become the rich, the exalted, and the honored.
The son of yon mean village-trader sits
Among the honored nobles of the realm,
Or 'mid a mighty nation's senators;
While some proud scion of a titled race
Beneath his influence an outcast dies,
Lost in Siberian realms of penury.

He came to me!—I held her hands in mine;
Her look of beauty met my enraptured gaze;
And as the rainbow, weaved in misty air,
In unmarked blending meets the meaner light,
So love, the link, the lustre of her look,
Leapt to my heart-glance and entwined us one.
Thus blissful, heedless of Time's presence, I
Basked in her beauty, bathed in streams of love;
All confident the clouds that speck life's sky
Could ne'er disturb, ne'er cast their shadows there.
But Time outspake: "Thy fond security,
Thy fancied joy I will all scatter soon!
Aye, hold her hand, and press it tenderly;
For that white hand shall cease to feel thy grasp,
Be there, while thou art far away with others.
Yea, 'tis the last, last precious time for years,
And then but once, when the fair fingers frail
Shall clasp thee with their ebbing warmth awhile,
Who (long in exile 'mid enjoyments new)
Shalt strangely taste again thine early bliss,
Whose harvest-hours had long since passed away."
But I in wrath, yet half in fear, outspake:

"I scorn thee, Time! and all thy bitter threats;
I do defy thy might to sever that
Which nought but Death's keen hand can break or
mar.
I do defy thee, thy predictions curse!"

I knew no more; one fierce triumphant glance,
And I lay writhing, all undone, half-senseless,
Despising life, like dungeoned captive, deep
In densest gloom of trouble, praying death!

But pity now, his rage outspent, returned;
And Time he took me gently in his arms;
And as the nurse, to still the children's cries,
Finds other toys for those all broken ones,
Which screaming angrily they push away—
So poured he then fresh treasures in my lap,
That I would hate still, vainly sighing for
The star now shining far above my reach.
But Time he wooed me still, and weaned me first
To take quiescent, then to love a little,
When most 'twas like the dear delight of yore,
And then to fondle on its own account;
And so to others; thus to taste once more,
And quaff deep draughts of bliss so strangely sweet,
That too soon stole that long-loved taste away—
For Time he knew his story to be true;
And so it proved, though I defied his power.
For Time he mouldeth other images
And rears them as the prized of old hath been.

Then I grew vexed, dispirited, unquiet;
Unfathomed feelings foaming in my breast;
Distrusting all, suspicious of myself;
Deeming the cherished, fondled, of to-day,
Might be to-morrow spurned and cast aside
For newer playthings. Half despising Time,
And yet half grateful for his later gifts.
I could not sorrow—had I not such joys?
I could not joy—I yearned for the old sorrow.
And so I paused, reluctant and perplexed,
While time with smiling mien still beckoned on—
When lo! before me stood a Form majestic,
Yet kind and gentle—and that great magician,
That all-tyrannic ruler of the earth,
Bent low before a Mightier One than he;
Who gently spake: "Why fearful and perplexed,
Dreading the operations of his hand
Whose work is Mine? My faithful servant he,
My minister and embassy to man.
Seest thou not himself he humbleth now?
Though all mysterious and tyrannic here,
There's not the meanest change his hand effects,
But what I order and I bring to pass;
'Tis noted all and registered in heaven.
Would'st thou he led thee through the sunny bay,
Just coursed the storm, and wooed the fairway bright,
Nor through the chequered roads 'mid rocks and shoals
And heaving treacherous channels guided thee?
I need but say the word, and this should be.

But lo! o'er fitful changing seas of life
Tost are her barks upon the boundless shore,
Left on eternity's vast tracts, but wrecks!
What matters then, whate'er the voyage may be,
If such its ending? But there is a river
(Take, use this glass, and thou shalt well discern it;
Use it whene'er thy heart shall faint and fail thee)—
Through rocks of giant-height deep, calm, and wide,
Runs up the land to My all-glorious haven,
The matchless city of that unknown clime,
The anchorage in a crystal waveless sea.
And I can bid Time safely bring thee there,
If thou wilt only trust in my sure hands
The voyage thy bark must make a little while."
He ceased. I answered: "Lord! all fearless now
I'll sail through changing seas, whate'er betide;
For in the tempest and the fleeting calm
I'll through this glass with joy behold my home,
While Thine unerring hand safe guideth me
Through that dark rocky pass, thence up the river,
Into Thy haven of eternal calm."
I ceased, looked up—and lo! I saw none near;
But the old man and I stood all alone.
Yet now no more in fear, but all in peace
And trustingly I took his hand in mine;
And he still leads me, by what way I know not,
But this I know: the minister safe guideth
Me onward to his Sovereign. When no more
The pilot needed, I shall calmly rest
Beside his throne, Lord of all earth and heaven.

METEOROLOGICAL ANNALS.

Winter 1858-9.

The snow-king stole out before his time,
For the lands lay yet in their autumned hue,
And the sun had not sought his own loved clime,
When the cold blast beneath him blew;
For sweet Summer had reigned oh! so lovely and
well,
And her days were so bright and long and clear,
That envious Winter would fain have his spell;
So he sent out his ice-winds drear,
While Autumn still lingered here!
But she drove him back to his frozen shore,
And he came not forth that winter more.
But when far and wide did the cold blasts go—
E'en Italia's sun-clime scare—
I looked for the terrible reign below,
That should still soft Grecia's blue waves' flow,
And bind in cold fetters of ice and snow,
Europa's south lands fair;
For if her sun-climes grew cold so soon,
What should our north isle do?
What hope from a warm wind's western boon,
That the merciless king chilled too?

So I waited long months of frost and snow—
How little we know! how little we know!—
And victor Autumn reigned, wreathed with flowers,
And a laurel of deathless green;
And the ice-wind fled from her zephyred bowers—
So reigned on the Conqueror Queen;
She outlived her foeman, the Polar King,
And died in the arms of her child, the Spring.

" 'Twill soon be wintered, that hope of ours!
For its leaves already are mellowed and sered,
And a chilled breath brushes its tender flowers."
Thus wait we the ill, thus the worst is feared—
When hope to our sered hearts comes, scares the ice-chain,
And our joys bud out into Spring again!

THE SORTIE.

MARCH 30, 1859.

VAINLY the winter-king strove to kill
Autumn's calm spirit that lingered still;
Low 'mid our island-haunts she hovered,
And the loaded fruit-boughs and hedge-rows covered
In rich-hued mantle of mellowing green,
From the withering frost-garb's snow-white sheen.
For she scared the stern lord of the north away,
And safe in her zephyred bower she lay;
But she died at length, when her child, the Spring,
Grew a ripening, fair, but still weak young thing.
Then roused up the pole-king his dormant strength,
Though defied so long, he would reign at length!
Tho' brief be his rule, all cruel and stern,
Till the summer-sun's troop-beams of light return,
To revenge his defeat, to efface his shame,
To strengthen his might, to recover his fame,
He would fill with ruin the balmy air,
And the glories of Spring should be blighted and
bare!
So he marshalled his icy storm-blasts wild,
And he rode forth to crush the stripling child.
On, at his beck, from the frost-bound coast
They *rush, that* fierce and pitiless host!

From the snow-waste climes of an unpierced shore,
From the ice-berged straits of Labrador,
From the chained sea-plains of endless white,
Where he rears his throne in the halls of night,
From Greenland's mountains of fathomless snow,
From where Iceland's chill waves forbear to flow,
They come, 'neath a cloud-garb of flaky snows!
And the Zephyr-Queen quakes, for his coming she knows.
Sweet nurse of the Spring Child! she fed him each day,
And long in her soft warm lap he lay;
In her fond embrace, by her balm-showers nourished,
Oh! well had the Spring Child grown and flourished!
And dire was the work of that terrible day,
When the Zephyrs awhile stole affrighted away.
But the Spring he grew bold, and with courage strong,
Though dire was the contest that boded long,
He faced the stern foe, till his faithful ally,
Recovering, swept on in her car through the sky,
And the boastful Winter beheld and fled,
And the victor Spring stood alone with his dead—
The vanquisher, yet the vanquished!

There lie they, all strewn on the snow-tinged ground,
The earlier hopes round that child-heart wound—
The young peach-blossom, the pear-bud gay,
The flow'ret of promise—all withered away!
For like tyrant, strong in merciless fight,
Is the harsh Spring-frost of a single night.

Weep, Spring! weep on thy woodland slopes!
Weep for the loss of thy budded hopes!
Let thy soft shower-drops on those sered leaves lie;
Wake them to blossom, that bent to die.
Let thy balm rain-tears on the dead plants fall—
A glistening, sun-gemmed funeral pall.

Shout, Spring! shout in thy sunny glades!
Smile, Spring! smile in thy violet shades!
Let them trill thy triumph, those birds of air;
And thy joy-strains bid the breezes bear.
Let the brooklet's babbling, the rippling rill,
Thy realms with the tale of thy conquests fill.
And, Zephyr! go tell, in thy southern home,
Of thine unmatched mission: how dared not come—
Whilst thou defiant didst choose to stay—
The Polar Tyrant, quite kept at bay.
Go, kiss the Gulf Stream that gave thee birth;
Tell of its triumphing over the earth—
Of an empire enlarged, where thine embassies went—
Of Winter chased off, to his exile-haunts sent;
How he dared not, this year, where thou wert, come—
Of a new clime allied to thy southern home!

Are the fair scenes of fortune now sunning our heart?
Does the sunshine of summer-hope its brightness im-
part?
Do we reap the rich fruits of our fondest desires,
Gay bask 'neath our joy-sun's meridian fires?
Do *we roam in* prosperity's luxuriant bowers?

O ye who thus thrive in life's gay summer hours!
Are those buds all matured that your early spring
nursed?
Are ye sipping the sweets that flowed fresh from the
first?
Were there no cherished saplings, that promised so
well,
'Neath experience's chill wind that blighted soon fell?
Did Hope's gentle zephyr ne'er steal her away,
And Despair's cutting blast never reign for one day?
Alas! all our fruitage ne'er blossomed on these,
But we ne'er gathered aught from those young Eden-
trees!
Our summer may be bright, and our sun may be high,
Our joys may be many—yet who thinks with no sigh,
On fair plants of promise in life's young spring time,
That the world's chill wind blighted, laid bare in their
prime?
Yet, patience! though hopes we once prized are no
more,
Perchance for life's harvest are others in store;
At least there is one which shall ever grow green,
Whate'er be the season on life's changing scene.

WINTER, 1859—60.

Now for the contest! The battle-field where?
Spot seldom sullied by strife of mankind—
This the arena for the foes of the air,
Fit field for the combat, when wind meets with
wind.

Over the ocean, and swelling in strength,
Rush the rough breezes, once gentle and kind;
For the blast of the north is returning at length;
He has weaved his ice-fetters the south shores to
bind.

No longer all smiles, with the wavelets at play,
That once leaped to kiss the bland breeze as she
passed—
The obstinate waters are torn into spray,
And they heave in the fury and wrath of the blast.

And the storm-stricken mariner kneels on the shore,
Who has weathered the tempest unscathed and
unharmed;
For he views the strewn timbers that ne'er as of yore
Shall sail, the blithe bark, when the billows are
calmed!

And he thinks of the men that lie mute in that bed,
Where the roar of the hurricane waned on their ear;
There's a terrible calm in those depths where they sped,
Though the fringe of their sea-shroud the storm-fiends may tear.

But the wind leaps to land! She has grappled the foe;
And a contest commences whose rigor and length
The records of this recent winter shall show—
Unexampled for years in duration and strength.

There's a stern stolid force in the breath of the one,
Like the calm man of muscle, secure in his power;
But the other grows great in her fury alone,
That once flitted lightly from bower to bower.

They have closed in their wrestling; now one has the day,
And the other a moment drops panting and crushed;
But he rallies his forces in fiercer array,
And the vanquisher's roar of defiance is hushed.

And the one chills the other; for scarce may ye say
That this is the wind from the land of the light!
And the rain-drops that fall from her store-clouds by day,
Grow frosted and hard in the folds of the night.

But yet not the victor, nor able to bind;
The chains of the pole-king are hoary and damp,
And his rough breath is wet with the warmth of the
wind
That rolls in from seaward, invading his camp.

And the sea-winds have torn his snow-mantle to
shreds;
And scarce is the fodder, and scanty the fare
For the cattle, all pining away in their sheds,
While the seeds rotting lie in the bleak barren air.

This then is the contest; the battle-field—where?
Spot that the foemen of earth dare not tread;
Yet it lies 'neath the contest all withered and bare,
Like the climes that the fierce tides of war have
o'erspread.

Early Autumn commenced it, and late in the Spring
Found the fight still unfinished, both combatants there;
But the sun shall advance with his troop-beams, and
bring
Victorious the Summer Queen his triumph to share

(For the Spring Infant—born in the thick of the
fray,
When the battle waxed fiercest—had died at its
birth;
He was reared not to drive the chill pole-king away,
The gloom of whose tyranny shaded the earth).

But higher and higher triumphant his march;
With a thousand balm-zephyrs that leap from the sea,
Uprides the bright orb over heaven's sapphire arch;
Though the winter long linger, soon, soon shall it flee.

At last—yes, at last the rough pole-king rolls back!
At length is the Summer Queen's victory won;
And the lone wind, left lingering late on the track,
Has gone round to be warmed in the light of the sun.

ROUND WITH THE SUN.

The wind, the last left of his winterly race,
Cast his cold icy mantle o'er valley and plain;
And the flowers they closed at his chilling embrace,
And nature she drooped in her dreary domain.

Yet—like tyrant-usurper, unloved and unblest,
With his subjects at variance, with favorites none—
The wind he soon wished he had hied with the rest,
When his race to their own polar regions had gone.

For he longed to rove blithely in nature's gay bowers,
To kiss the young violet, and toy with the trees,
To go courting a thousand sweet blossoming flowers,
And not to be shunned so by all that he sees.

So he fixed his resolve in the stern morning grey,
And he carried it out ere the day was half done;
So slyly and surely the wind stole away,
And went round to be warmed in the light of the
sun.

And he came back a zephyr all balmy and bright!
Then the flowers unfolded their leaves as he passed,
And the trees nodded kindly, arrayed in their white;
So the wind was contented and happy at last.

Am I gloomy and cheerless, with manners uncouth,
Unpleasant my speech, and all bitter its tone?
'Twere well to be sure of and grieved at the truth—
Let me, too, turn round, like the wind, to the sun.

Is my character harsh, is my conduct unkind?
Am I losing all friends, growing welcome to none?
Then let me betimes become wise like the wind,
Turn round to be warmed in the light of the sun.

Have I long been reserved, and from others estranged?
In life's earlier hours, ere her day is half done,
Let me, like the wind, just be sure I am changed,
That I, too, at length have gone round with the sun.

SUMMER, 1860.

THE Zephyr was proud of her prowess and might,
When she coped with the chilling ice-blast,
And vanquished the veteran winter king quite,
Reposing victorious at last.

Yet she seldom was feared, few her presence would
awe—
She was loved as the gentle and mild—
She would wish to be dreaded by all that she saw;
Like the north blast, a tyrant as wild!

So she threw off her mantle of sunshine, and rose
To the height of her fury and powers;
You'd have fancied her leagued with the icebergs and
snows,
And not with the sun and the flowers!

For she washed out her warmth in the depths of the
main,
And wailed as she whirled it on high;
For her own pleasure now were the waves lashed
again
As before, when the winter was nigh.

And she rolled up the waters in masses of black,
That should shut out each soft summer ray,
And, spread round about her, move on in her track,
To scare the bright sunbeams away.

And the shadows above fall to darken man's mind,
Like the damp earth, and moist dripping trees;
In place of the summer he waited to find—
Bright sunshine, and soft balmy breeze.

There is cloud in the sky when the sun has uprisen,
And the landscape looks saddened and drear;
But the drops that fall loosed from their vapory
prison,
May make not the leaden sky clear.

And the long summer twilights look sullen, and die
All rayless—the grove walks are wet
And deserted; and lovers impatiently sigh
For the rambles they never can get.

Now the sun at the zenith is turning away,
To close the disastrous campaign;
For the wind and the sea they have kept him at bay,
With their armies of cloud and of rain.

Nor clearer, nor softer the shortening eves;
More dim into darkness they fall;
Now Autumn comes on — are they mildewed, her
sheaves?
Who broods not of scarceness at all?

Be proud then, O Zephyr! thy conquest is won;
But its object — what! fortune unkind?
Does every one sigh for a sight of the sun,
Yet none give one thought to the wind?

Despised, disregarded, her might unapproved,
None renders her homage or fear.
O Zephyr! much better have reigned to be loved
In thy balm, as on each former year.

The north 'tis his sphere (and we give him his due
For), the stern, stately, chilling, and grand;
But the sunny south-west, if her mission be true,
Should be rather the balmy and bland.

And we all love the Zephyr; but why is it so?
The cause is, methinks, just this one:
That laden with sunbeams her balmy wings glow,
That she's a true child of the sun.

But if she turn errant and wayward and wild,
And throw off the yoke she best bore,
We deem her, then, just an undutiful child,
And she gains our affection no more.

There are zephyrs on earth — yes, perchance this is
so! —
Discontented to reap merely love,
Are coveting more like cold north winds to grow;
How vain, too, *their* efforts must prove!

True, they work out their ends, all their loveliness
lose;
But what for their pains is their gain?
To all but the *real* men their homage refuse;
Who quit their own spheres work in vain.

Can the summer be winter? the south be the
north?
Or the storm prove as though it were still?
Shall the day in the garment of night issue forth?
Or the valley rise high as the hill?

They who ape other's manners, we soon recognise
How it never becomes them at all;
And we yield them no homage, but rather despise—
Such attempts to be great prove but small!

Stay then, zephyrs of earth! and if such be your
sphere,
Ere a course quite as futile ye run,
Remember, the sunny south-wind proved but dear
As a faithful ally of the sun.

WINTER, 1860—1.

THE wintry wind that wooed the sea, and shunned the sunshine fair,
And girt herself with cold grey clouds that chilled the summer air,
The watery wind had dropped at length, and slunk away ashamed,
And the polar blast, all unopposed, his full possession claimed.
Yet when with mantling garb of snows and fettering frosts he flew,
We calmly waited winter-time, as though 'twere nothing new;
We did not know, though, what his sway all undisturbed could be,
Or how he reigns, unthwarted by the breezes from the sea.
Yet thus he came, and o'er the land dispersed his forces white;
And the little rivulet dared dance no longer in the light;
All hushed the songs of triumph that the rains had taught the rill,
And, save the wailing of the wind, all nature's voice *grew still.*

But e'en he scorned not beauty, nor stood leagued
against the sun,
But terms of peace concluded — thus did the treaty
run:
Content but be the latter to remain beyond where
ends
His northern frontier, then they both might jointly
act as friends.
So, as if to shame the zephyr, who had lost both
light and balm,
The pole-king in his fiercest hour had left us much
to charm.
We strolled forth that same morning, when his reign
was at its height,
And lo! the distant landscape lay all bathed in
silvery light!
And the trees, though they had lost their green, were
hung with crystal gems,
And far more numerous than spring-dews those crisp
snow-diadems.
And o'er the whitened meadows, 'cross the closely
nestling dells,
Was floated far and wide the cry of village Christmas
bells.
For though the blood shrunk sluggish in these human
veins of ours,
Man by exertion quells the cold, defies the tyrant
powers;
And so when nature drooping lies all prostrate on
her earth,

Each human heart undaunted vies in social acts of mirth.
We walked in light, we walked on light, light everywhere around;
Bright beamed the sun, bright seemed the air, and brightly flashed the ground!
What could we want more beautiful? Yet were we then content?
Nor onward to a future spring our wayward fancies went?
Light lacking heat—oh, lovely is the lengthening light of day!
And beautiful the soft white beam of nature's earliest ray!
Yet hear her teachings: though her landscape stretch away so fair,
Her beauties are but half complete, if warmth be wanting there;
And though upon her cold white gems the lengthening sun-rays fall,
One soft warm blush of tender spring is better far than all.

But the pole-king now, his rage appeased, regains his northern track;
And the zephyrs (though so young the year) are blithely bounding back,
To woo at will the sunshine, or to court the balmier showers,
While scarce one stray north-blast returns to scare *the* ripening flowers.

All freely sport the zephyrs, while the advancing
sunbeams fling
Each day's increasing load of balm, and make them
meet for spring.
And now along the fresh green fields, adown the
sunny vales,
The breath of spring comes floating with the fitful
April gales;
And violets in the shaded ways their perfumed
incense bring,
And budding forests once again their first young
shadows fling;
And flowers unblighted, growing bold, have reared
their heads to sing,
And nature's song is borne aloft by birds upon the
wing;
And through renewed creation lo! the swelling
anthems ring;
The harshest winter hours may yield the brightest
earliest spring!
While zephyrs, robed in richest balm, waft far and
wide the song,
As though to amend their past misdeeds, atone their
last year's wrong.

"Wrong," did I say? I did—and yet I know there
are no flaws—
No, not the slightest to be found in nature's perfect
laws.

Wrong!—I but uttered fables when I sketched a
tale of strife,
As though with man's discordant deeds God's very
heaven were rife.
Wrong!—let me cast them down at once, those
fabrics I have reared;
Suffice, if 'mid their shadowy ways some ray of
truth appeared.
Let these poor pictures pass away of a would-be
poet's brain,
If but—more fitting things to stay—some lessons
taught remain.

Hear then these last: There's nought can clash in
nature's wide domain;
There's nought discordant can disturb her most har-
monious reign.
The winds from north and south that blow have each
their work assigned;
The elements no variance know—wind cannot war
with wind.
Why now the ocean-breezes bring a winter wet and
mild,
Or waft away the summer heats with gales prolonged
and wild,
Veiling the noontide splendor with dark clouds of
chilling rain—
Such knowledge is too wonderful, we cannot yet
attain.

Why now the icy blast returns all gloomily severe,
And in a pall of whited snows wraps round the dying year,
While the new one quickly following, all blithesomely may bring
An unexpected season mild, a soft and genial spring,
And perchance a summer glowing bright with sunshine from on high –
That these things may be, this we know; we do not yet know why.
What imaged by mere mortal acts may dire confusion seem
(Such are the pictures drawn by man, the poet's fancied dream),
What only seems a season marred to our short seeing eyes,
Are workings of some all-wise law that from us hidden lies—
Whether the soft sweet sunshine cheers or rains unwearying fall—
For the Great God who reigns above hath ordering of it all.

'Tis but, alas! with humankind, where sin and error stain,
And laws *are* broken, that confusion and disorder reign;
And men with men at variance grow, in stubborn strife engage,
And *human blood* is made to flow, and wars and *tumults* rage.

Yet ever here, 'mid sickening scenes of sin and wild unrest,
Lo! the same Lord of nature orders all things for the best.
Then be not mute, ye saddened ones, whom winter-griefs have bound,
And troubles chillier than the snows and sorrows sore surround!
Go, whisper to your fainting hearts—and that shall solace bring:
On grief's severest winter-night may dawn the earliest spring!

What, silent! ye who sometime since 'neath clouds of sorrow lay,
From whom dark winter-time rolled off — returned joy's spring-time gay!
Deaf are ye unto nature's praise? What! hear ye not her voice?
Will ye not, too, your voices raise, with all her works rejoice?
Go, with the fresh young violets your grateful incense bring;
Mount up, O souls, in ecstacies with birds upon the wing!
Yea, with God's glad creation let your swelling anthems ring;
For have not grief's most wintry hours brought brightest, loveliest Spring?

DESCRIPTIVE PIECES.

THE HILL RANGE,

AS VIEWED FROM BARNSBURY AND HIGHBURY.

How sweet at eventide to gaze
Upon those green slopes graced with wood,
When amber garb of sunset haze
Has wrapped them round with golden flood!

Look down, dear range of hills! look down,
And smile on this my native place;
Green girdle of the giant town!
I love thy soft wood sides to trace.

The still groves looked on Albion's pride;
Alarmed her crowded haunts they viewed;
So clung they to the high hill side
Above that mighty multitude.

The town-arched sky—with leaden hue,
Far o'er a thousand chimney tops,
That dulled its depthless sea of blue—
Relieved, on thy sweet summit drops.

Her noonday sun grew dull and dim,
All vain essayed 'mid smoke to shine;
But reached at length thy verdant rim,
And kissed that breezy brow of thine!

Along in haste the fleece-clouds flew—
Too soon they catch the sombre stain;
But past thy cool refreshing dew
They sail with snow white tints again.

A thousand toil-worn, pale-faced men
From stifling haunts gaze up at thee,
And rural grove, and shaded glen,
Like some sweet Eden-sight, they see!

I've roamed through beauty's richer tracks,
Where every nook her graces fill;
But many a rural landscape lacks
Thy gentle charm, sweet range of hill!

The usurper town with might came forth,
And from his grasp the green meads flee;
But stand they fearless toward the north,
And bivouac peacefully with thee.

And still that life-tide rolls along,
Till thou their pierceless bound shalt be;
For thou shalt stem that myriad throng,
As some tall cliff defies the sea!

Once sister heights embraced thy feet,
And to thy sides young green slopes clung,
Where the bright babbling brooks would meet,
That rippling through those still vales sung.

Now formal Art reigns gravely, on
Sweet spots where Nature revelled free;
And town-tied, captured Islington
Has one joy left—to gaze on thee!

So from her haunts—my native place—
With changed emotions in my breast,
I've loved thy fringe of green to trace,
Till, like yon orb, my heart found rest.

Time was, when undisturbed around
Slope answered slope with rural breath;
And still wood nooks an echo found,
'Cross patches of untrodden heath.

But on the varying plains of time
Lo! Art and Commerce march along;
Arcadia quits her traitor clime,
With all her sweet array of song.

And vanquished Nature quick retreats
And flees the haunts she loved so well;
And long, dull lines of formal streets
Creep up the hill and fill the dell.

But I ne'er knew thee, native place!
The "merrie" village of the past,
In thy yonng charms and rural grace—
My lot in later times is cast.

Yet not my careless infant hours,
But visioned realms of golden youth
Made all thy haunts enchantment's bowers,
Sweet, fabling unattractive truth.

And I have roamed thy brick-lined ways,
And sauntered in each rigid square;
But, through young Love's illusive haze,
Birds, flowers, and fields were round me there!

And empty names of places mean
Acquired real charms in youth's gay eye,
Stood clothed with verdant tracts of green,
As though bright brooks still babbled by.

Thus in life's morning-mist-clouds lay
Sweet sylvan scenes of splendor rare;
But noontide rolled the clouds away,
Disclosed a vast dull region there!

Life's rules and truths and trials came,
And bricked up hopes that gambolled free;
And sterner knowledge dulled the flame
Of young Love's unsuspecting glee.

But—dried my tears—I've gazed on thee
In calm of sunny eventide,
And those sweet sun-rays gladdened me
That flood with light thy wooded side.

And those thy eve-illumined spires,
High nestling 'mid their native wood,
Breathed hopes of holier heart-desires,
Of some celestial, deathless good.

And as, on thy high ridges reared,
They seemed to kiss the azure sky,
Did they not waft sweet hopes that cheered,
Based upon ground as firm and high?

Ye sons of Islington! who here
Have grasped youth's sweets that slipped away,
Oh let that wood-range prospect cheer,
Viewed mellowing 'neath some sunset ray!

Then picture life no dull flat plain,
But with some nobler deeds reared high;
Some verdant, hill-abiding chain,
That travellers in her vales descry.

And may—'mid landscapes of the past—
Youth's lost joys lie on memory's slope,
O'er duller tracts their charms to cast,
When dimmed the distant heights of Hope!

THE ISLE OF WIGHT.

THE children of Nature—her scenic delights—
All disputing, each scorned to abide with the rest;
So they every one spread them o'er various sites,
And they all scampered off to north, south, east, and
west.

The bold, wild, and barren refused to remain
With the soft and the gentle, the cultured and fair;
And the sky-piercing snow-peaks had looked with
disdain
On the timid green slopes, that dared scarce kiss the
air.

But Nature, all wise, gathered up in her arms,
And bound with blue girdle of soft swelling sea,
A sample of each of her runaway charms,
To a spot where each linked to the others should be.

The bold and the rocky, the sterile and wild,
With a tinge of the lofty, romantic, and grand,
And much of the pretty and rural and mild—
She would mingle them all in this fair Eden-land!

Towering cliffs, and sharp headlands, and rocks
many hued,
Here scattered chaotic, there blending sublime;
Now verdant with foliage, with fair flowrets strewed,
Like the beautiful nurslings of soft southern clime!

And green swelling downs that, compared to the
size
Of the coast they keep guard on, might mountains
appear;
From whose heather-waved summits we well recog-
nize
The sweet, gentle, rural—wild, sterile, and drear.

Here are silver-twined rivers, and green shelving
shores,
Noble bays and dark headlands spread forth into
sight;
For nature unlocks here her cabinet-stores
Of beauty and grandeur in the fair Isle of Wight!

Sweet starlet of Ocean! dear Albion's delight!
Methinks all her wide-spreading charms meet in thee!
Thou dost nestle beside her, her loved satellite,
By the west breezes wooed, and embraced by the sea.

And oft, when the heart of the nation beats low,
Or fevered with strife, or tumultuous with care,
Its Life-Stream apart from intrusion shall flow,
Nor grief be lashed wild in thy soft soothing air.

Howe'er the fierce waves not e'en monarchs can
stay,
May have left the wide shore but a waste barren
track,
In the shrine of thy sea-palace, each hallowed day
'Mid the charms of thy shores wafts a comforter
back!

Now Nature she needed the muse's soft lay,
And the spirit of poesy in some master mind,
To feast on the fair scenes around him that lay,
Fit food for his fancies and song themes to find.

So she sought for and gained the best bard in our
land,
And she stationed him here, 'mid the wild and the
still;
And she bade him her services daily command
On the green grassy slope-downs of Freshwater Hill.

I have viewed thy fair land, Bard! nor wonder that
thou,
So gifted by Nature, so graced by her here,
Inspiration shouldst sip on that silent hill brow,
That should thrill through our hearts when thy
pages appear.

For me—just one brief blissful glance, and I go,
To a less grateful task, to my every-day sight;
Yet like nectar to sweeten life's currents shall flow
Thy cherished remembrance, fair island of Wight!

RAMSGATE.

THE rough waves rolled on the shelving shore,
Their own old ocean's ambassage;
And they tribute claim for the monarch hoar,
To woo his smiles and to calm his rage;
And the white foam falls on the red-hued sand,
And moans to the monarchs of the land.

First Grandeur stalked with gigantic stride,
And uttered proudly, "I (meet for thee)
Will rear the rough rock by thy restless side,
All calm 'mid thy rage, impatient sea!
And my wild barren mountains that pierce the sky
If thou wilt, shall court thee—if not, defy!"

Next wild Romance, with her wanton mien,
Now fruitful and shaded, now stern and bare,
Flung round the sea-king her fitful scene,
And rock, river, mountain, and dell are there;
And thick wood-slopes with their sylvan grove,
And the crest of the hill-peak high above!

And her sister, Beauty, is there as well,
Where the hill-slopes soften, and green trees twine,
And *silvery streams* from her silent dell

Smile, widening to blend with his breast of brine.
She wears no mien of defiant pride,
For she loves to be linked to his cherished side.

There wait they, all circling our island home—
Dear spots, where old ocean loves to come!—
There build they their throne by the briny tide,
Those chieftains of Nature, her grace and pride!
And the billows rise, and the billows swell,
And leap on the land they love so well.

Seek Wales, if you prize my first the most,
Or the rough barren rock of our northern coast;
But where lurk the other two, ask you? Where
As in Devon's soft clime of beauty rare;
While yon young isle, broke loose from the parent beach,
Methinks boasts a sample share of each.

But lo! from the land I see her rise,
The maiden gay with the glistening eyes!
She, too, to the hoar king's side would press,
And they call her the virgin Cheerfulness.
Sorrow and pain from her presence flee;
All smiling she stands beside the sea.

With a merry motley group she comes—
The haggard escaped from their close town-*homes*—

On that frail face flickers the smile of yore;
And the slave of commerce has left his store;
And anger and crime grow good and kind,
For they leave the haunts of their sin behind.

There are smiles that for once are heart-notes gay,
And sweet mirth sinless awhile holds sway;
And the young with the young sweet converse share—
One warrior alone with his dart is there,
Who glories in greater might to be,
Where the gay sylph courts the treacherous sea!

Now ask you again of the spot where most
The mirth-sprite hies on our island coast,
Where her votaries hurry in thronging trains,
And the pallid townsman forgets his pains?
Go question some one of those youthful bands,
And, lisping, they tell you of Ramsgate Sands.

If nought else had courted thee, nymph of the sea!
Methinks not unprized in our heart thou'dst be;
But the other land-queens ne'er scorned thee quite,
For the green fields are waved o'er thy chalk cliffs
white;
And beauty bends low o'er thy thronged haunts gay,
And the soothed sea smiles in thy summer ray!

SUNSET ON THE SEA.

ILFRACOMBE.

On the edge of the ocean the sun was careering,
But the warmth of his brightness had fled from the
hill;
While there, like some dream of the past disappearing,
On that far distant verge he is lingering still!

In the valley the glow of his flushings had faded,
And the dim hills girt round them their mantle of
brown;
But still, to my fancy, the waves he evaded—
Pale and chilled by the sea-mists—yet would not go
down!

On that raw summer eve, musing silent and pensive
(As my vision discerned, when the sun sank at last,
A faint glory, unfelt here): Are views so extensive
Within the best radius of loveliness cast?

And may not the flood-tide of beauty set stronger,
Where the wood-heights catch waiting the last shower
of red,
As he leans from above to their breast, soon no longer
Beheld, while his troop-beams lie marshalled o'erhead?

So may not a circumscribed range shed a splendor,
Where a wide penetration, to mortal eye weak,
The distance may not of its lustre, and render
Some bright bar of light but a colorless streak?

Not in vain, not in vain! Though the barrier be nigh us,
Though curtailed be our sphere, and our influence slight,
There are fields for our care and our culture lie by us—
Truth, beauty, and love can shed round us their light!

ILFRACOMBE.

Close your eyes, my friend! and view
High peaked hills that front the sea,
Clothed with green of varying hue—
Furze and meadow, wheat and tree—
Shelving down on either side,
Heights descend on heights, and vales
Quit the hill-breasts and their pride,
Slipping softly to the dales,

On whose infant slopes the woods
In their park-like beauty fall
Graceful to the streamlet floods
In the dells more meek than all.
Sometimes, though, the haughty hill
Proudly scorns the timid valley—
Stands above, unbending still,
Where his bold attendants rally;
There the precipices steep,
And the cliffs and gorges wild
Hang above the ravine deep.
She, the untamed, ungentle child,
Lacks her sister's grace and sweetness,
Lacks her tender charms and fair,
Shews for sterner aspects meetness.
But the whole in its completeness
Weaves a spell of beauty, where
Nature counts such treasures rare,
Varied, rich beyond compare!
Let your inland thoughts with fleetness
To this famed sea-haunt repair;
Then return, and say, "'Tis there!"

BILLOWS ON THE GRAIN

ILFRACOMBE.

HARMLESS swellings on the grain,
Gentle waves that sweep the hill,
While the harsh winds lash the main;
Corn-ears, bending meek and still,
On a hundred hill-slopes sown,
Where dark knolls of woodland charm,
And the loftier chains look down,
In their barren sternness calm!
Thus earth's fruit up toward the sun
Stretches, golden garb to don,
Meekly bears the cloud-shades dun,
Bends while howling gales roll on.
Treacherous, silent, silvery sea!
Slothful sleeping in the sun,
While the winds a moment flee—
What of thy work—hast thou none?
When the blast returning blows,
Sweeping o'er thy breadth of main,
Thee (who vainly darest to oppose)
He shall lash to foam again!

And a thousand ills shall rise,
Brooding o'er thy heaving flood,
When thou warrest with the skies—
Worse than strife of human blood.

As fair fields that slope on high,
Flashing with the golden grain—
'Spite the frownings of the sky,
Meekly drinking in the rain;
Calm while cloud-shades flit along,
Bowing softly to the blast;
Rustling to the sun their song—
So they yield rich stores at last:

So, my soul! look thou to heaven;
From hope's crest thy fruit prepare;
Let thy daily life be given
Grain of grace and love to bear.
Then if winds of trouble rage,
Humbly bowing 'neath the yoke,
Peaceful thou no war shalt wage,
Calm beneath affliction's stroke;
Smiling in the sunlit hour,
Drinking in grief's needful rain;
Trouble's waves shall lose their power—
Harmless billows on the grain!

MOUNTAIN SHEEP.

COMPOSED AT LLANDUDNO, NORTH WALES.

WHERE on either side the bay,
Flings its blue waves on the land,
And the heights in stern array
One against the other stand—
Far too fierce and sullen these,
As they proudly front the sea,
To be clothed with stately trees,
Or arrayed in woodland be!—
Yet save where bare rock throws out
Shadows on the meads below,
Gentle grasses all about,
Even to the summit, grow.
Then I climbed the steep hill-side,
High upon the summit lay;
Saw the heaving ocean wide,
Saw high mountains far away,
Saw flat meadow-land between
Height and height, and cheerful town
Filling up the wondrous scene,
'Neath the loftier hill-slope grown;
Heard alone the breezes, borne
From their accustomed haunt, the deep,

And the rustling of the corn,
And the bleating of the sheep.
Poor, mean, humble mountain sheep!
Type to us of all things low!
Yet ye scale the mountain steep,
Dwell upon the high hill brow;
While poor man on peopled plain,
Dead to nature's higher life,
Makes his all in this world's gain,
'Mid its cares and griefs and strife—
All earth's fleeting joys to gain,
All earth's rusting gold to keep—
Ne'er the hill-top cares to attain,
Lives below ye, mountain sheep!
True, ye live but to descend
From your native mountain home,
And, your short-lived days to end,
Soon unto the thronged towns come.
Yet, despised and humble sheep!
Only unto you 'tis given,
While you live, on mountain steep
To be living nearest heaven!
Then, like One I'd know and love,
For man's want and daily need
To descend from height above,
And for man a victim bleed.
And, if lives ye have, beside
That poor mangled body torn,
Ye shall seek your old hill side,
To your mountain top be borne!

Thus I mused upon the hill,
Morning blithe and hot noonday;
Saw the mountains dim and still,
Saw the frisking sheep at play;
Calmly stretched upon the height,
Saw the blue waves landward leap,
Saw on peak and slope the light,
Thought sweet thoughts of mountain sheep.

SONGS.

ENGLAND'S MELODIES.

DEAR England! are thy native glades
No nurslings of Apollo's art?
Ne'er waft they thro' dim history's shades
The strains thy first-born sons impart?
And do thy harp-strings silent lie,
Or but in borrowed notes arise?
Must we, thy sons, deploring sigh,
"Alas! she has no melodies?"

Nay, England, nay! thy fertile vales—
Each woodland slope, each grassy mead—
Waft nobler music with the gales,
There purer notes thy children read;
Each ivied tower, each gentle hill,
The woodlark's trill when morn is nigh,
With grander strains our bosoms fill—
Thy matchless songs of liberty!

NOT THAT SONG NOW.

Not that song now—for sorrow's touch
Hath tuned my heart to sadder strain,
And that which once could charm me much,
Seems joyless now, and fraught with pain.

Can the sweet sounds of balmy May
Be mingled with those calm delights
That gild the cold December day,
That gladden the dull winter nights?

So must this wintry heart, whose May
And gladsome spring have ceased to glow,
Forget each once-loved youthful lay
And list to other music now.

Another hand 'tis strikes the keys,
So other, newer strains must flow;
Then sing me, dearest! what you please—
But oh! not that—not that song now.

THE FIRST BLOSSOM.

WAS the herald of spring! the bright zephyr, that
flew
'om the sweet sunny south o'er the ocean of blue!
ill the trees were all bare yet, their snow-garb had
gone,
ıd but one little blossom was blooming alone.

Sweet sign of the summer! sweet blossom!" I said,
Like the dawning of life 'mid the haunts of the dead,
ke the first step of peace on the fields of the slain,
ıou dost whisper of fruit-time and harvest again!"

on laughed the gay spring loud through woodland
and mead,
ıd the blossoms around me in bright tints were
spread;
ıt the one that, ere spring came, had bloomed all
alone,
'as blighted and withered ere spring time had gone!

So soon the spring buddings of bright hopes appear,
Ere our young hearts have learnt the world's chill
winds to fear;
They were too fair to ripen, too child-like to stay,
So they blossomed a moment, then withered away!

TRUST NOT, OR TRUST.

Trust not, trust not the winning ones of earth!
Their looks are snares, their words soft music-notes;
Their smiles are but brief passing gleams of mirth,
Like sunlight on the silvery stream that floats.

Trust not those words that woo but for awhile,
Like sweet and soothing strains that die away;
Trust not, oh, trust not that bright beaming smile!
Nor credit vows but uttered to betray.

Trust not, trust not!—Oh, weak and foolish cry!
Shall disappointment dim earth's kindliest fire?
A few foes 'tis that make the coward fly;
At one repulse should valiant men retire?

Again advance with firmer, bolder tread;
Uplift love's lance in brighter, keener flame!
The hero on the battle-field that bled,
His wounds all healed, again fights on for fame.

Trust on, trust on! though faithless ones there be,
True, honest, heartfelt love shall not be vain;
Though disappointment vex and sadden thee,
Faint not, nor flee, but bold advance again!

Trust on, trust on! Amid that fitful hue,
Are starlight gleams, that time shall brighter prove;
Trust on, trust on! for loving hearts and true
Are dear rewards of those who dare to love.

THOSE HILLS BY THE SEASIDE.

Oh those hills by the seaside! how pleasant are they—
Where the soft zephyrs sigh, and the bright breezes
play,
Where the gay sunlight gleams on the low-lying
spray—
Oh those hills by the seaside! so pleasant are they!

Sweet hills by the seaside, so sunny and free!
Where the light waves came bounding across the blue sea,
While the rich woodland valleys were stretching away,
And the green grassy meadows in bright beauty lay!

I climbed the grey cliffs from the sand-shelving shore,
Where the billows were breaking in deep sullen roar,
Up that steep winding pathway where the wild flowers grow,
And the streamlet descends in light silvery flow.

And I sat on the summit when morning beamed bright,
And the gay tinted landscape lay bathed in the light;
And dear haunts and sweet spots all around could I see,
On those heights by the seaside, so cherished by me!

But those glad days of youth how they glided away!
And the bright hopes they fostered grew withered and grey;
So all that now gladdens is destined to flee—
Yet pleasant as ever those heights by the sea!

CITY CHARMS.

You may speak of sweet valleys, of grey mountain passes,
Where the red heather carpets the peak's rugged crest,
Of such grand charms of nature that nothing surpasses,
Where the foaming stream falls on the lake's glassy breast:
Though deserted by nature, yet spare me your pity!
I have sweets that she yields not my heart gathers here;
With my home and my hopes in the thick thronging city—
What haunts that ye tell of could time prove so dear?

Yes! 'tis pleasant, I know, 'mid the moorlands to travel,
And to scale the high hill tops, all blithesome and free;
But perchance I can charms that ye know not unravel,
That have grown in the heart of the city for me.

Though the close crowded streets have encompassed
my dwelling,
Have not sweet buds of childhood here peacefully
blown ?
Here are not the bright streams of youth's bliss out-
welling ?
Then go to your nature-charms, leave me my own !

LIGHTED LAMPS.

The lamps they were lighted
The first time at tea ;
And she was invited,
And sat next to me.
And the summer had flown
To the soft southern sky,
Yet still I must own
That happy was I !

We had many a party
Those winter nights gay ;
And I know how my heart I
Felt stealing away !

For I danced with that sweet one,
And home with her walked;
And, where we could meet none,
How gaily we talked!

The lamps they were lighted
No longer at tea;
For winter, affrighted,
Prepared quick to flee;
And the blossoms were blooming
On hedgerow and tree—
And my loved one was coming
To roam forth with me.

Then I told her I loved her,
When the summer sun shone,
And that evening we roved where
The trees meet, alone;
And the bees they were humming
In innocent glee,
When my own love was coming
To wander with me.

The autumn has tinted
With mellower hue—
What phantom has hinted
My loved one untrue?
The woods they grew golden,
The sun stole away—
Oh! sadly all told then
Of hopes that decay!

Now shorter each day grew,
Cold came on the nights,
Aud swiftly away flew
Those summer delights.
And she —— she had slighted
And wandered from me,
When the lamps next wère lighted
The first time at tea!

I DO NOT CARE TO ASK THEE NOW.

I do not care to ask thee now
If thou 'lt be mine, if thou 'lt be mine;
Nor 'mid the mists of pleasure's glow
Thy heart divine, thy heart divine.

But if a look, a word can be
To thee a sign, to thee a sign,
If aught I do betray to thee
That love of mine, that love of mine—

Then go thou forth, and ponder well
What thou wilt do, what thou wilt do;
What tale of love thy tongue shall tell,
When thee I woo, when thee I woo.

If I may know thee, love thee more
Than I do here, than I do here,
My fondest hopes I'll gladly pour
Into thine ear, into thine ear.

Not always sweet, or fond, or true,
Is pleasure's smile, is pleasure's smile;
I'd see thee 'neath some sunnier hue—
Then wait awhile, then wait awhile.

In rural scene, some calm retreat,
When none are near, when none are near,
And (quite by chance, of course) we meet,
I'll ask thee, dear, I'll ask thee, dear!

In some still nook, some shady glen
Where woods entwine, where woods entwine,
I'll roam with thee, and ask thee then
If thou 'lt be mine, if thou 'lt be mine!

DIE OUT!

DIE out— O Love!—this aching breast,
Where once grew fancied charms and good,
Where youth with silver mantle drest
And angelled common womanhood!

Reign in—O Love!—this hopeful heart,
Where virtue needs no mock disguise;
Where truth and piety impart
Real lustre to the glowing eyes.

Die out, where mere romance had weaved
To perfect bliss an earthly joy;
Reign in, where riper years conceived
Earth's best hopes stained with mixed alloy.

Die out young Love—that foolish thought—
Her way a smooth, wide road to heaven;
Reign in, that wise experience taught,
Poor gleam, to cheer earth's thorn-tracts given!

Reign in, where pure connubial sweet,
The patient bearing of earth's strife,
Where heavenward turned the willing feet
Give truest picture of a wife.

Die out, dulled dream of perfect form
(As tho' one heart were free from sin!);
Enduring Love! that still'st the storm
Of daily strife, reign in, reign in!

LOVE'S LABYRINTH.

No MORE; thy mazy paths, O Love!
Too oft I trod in younger days,
When lighter in life's morn I'd rove,
Bound thro' thy thorned and flowery ways!
No more thy mazy paths for me,
Or else I will not walk with thee!

Thy rugged road for me no more,
That tears afresh the aching heart—
I' ve had too much of this before;
Give me some level way to start!
Hew out a smoother road for me,
Or I will no more go with thee!

I' ll no soft eyes now gently glowing
And flashing fondness forth to-day,
To-morrow dull, cold, doubt-looks snowing,
Or turned to beam another way!
Play no such freaks, O Love! with me,
Or I will soon depart from thee.

Thy shifting scenes no more I'll wander,
Where cold estrangement's floods o'erflow,
And babbling brooks of bliss meander—
No varying course like this I'll go;
Find a more peaceful path for me,
Or I will have no more of thee!

THE RE-GATHERING SONG.

We viewed the rain-drops falling
On those dull wet autumn nights;
And the cherished past recalling
In that hour between the lights,
We thought of summer weather,
And that merry party, too,
When we gambolled on the heather,
As we gaily roamed with you.

Our homes looked dull and sad then,
The miry streets looked worse,
And notes of absence had then
Tolled round us like a curse!
And the wailing wind swept by us,
And the town-tree leaves fell dead,
And you, kind friends! once nigh us,
Like summer birds had fled.

But freed from your vocations,
We greet you each again;
Come, join our recreations,
Come, swell our festal strain!
While the fire is blazing brightly,
And shining on the wall,
We'll trip o'er the warm floor lightly,
United one and all.

And when, the sunbeams burning,
The fields shall woo us back,
We in this blithe dance turning,
Will away to the woodland track.
And may genial Christmas tether
Hearts no chill blast can blight,
That we roam again together,
In the gladsome summer light!

YOU NEVER CAME TO SAY GOOD BYE.

You never came to say good-bye,
Last autumn, when you went awáy:
'Twas thus we parted, you and I,
I vainly waiting all the day:
For much then drew my heart to thee;
Methinks one hour had sealed the spell—
But no! this was not so to be—
You never came to say Farewell.

Love's fuel, ready to ignite,
Time laid within this lonesome heart;
'Twas but for you to apply the light,
Your presence just the warmth to impart.
One gentle look had fanned the flame,
One little word like spark to fly—
But all in vain—you never came,
No! never came to say Good-bye!

I could not feed on far-off hopes,
When all unshaped, unhewn they lay;
Vague, shallow love too soon elopes;
Uncaged, the wild bird hies away.

You might around my heart have hung
That, time had failed to tear away;
But no—you left love's harp unstrung,
So other hands have tuned the lay.

And now you're standing by once more—
But so are other forms more dear;
All fled the hopes I nursed of yore,
That day I waited for you here.
You left the case unlocked, and lo!
Time too soon stole love's gem away!
No cherished parting hour!—and so
We meet all coldly here to day.

MY LITTLE THOUGHT.

A LITTLE thought came in my head;
It was so pleasant, that I said:
" This thought—it shall be reared and fed,
Till it shall ripen to a plan,
Just as the child becomes a man."
Too confident, I said " It can!"
I felt it ought.

Like little bird in parent nest,
My thought it throve within my breast,
Too premature to be exprest.
The fruitage-time of action nigh,
My thought it ripened but to die!
'Twas buried in my bosom's sigh—
Poor little thought!

A new idea I cherish now—
Nay, maiden! it must secret grow,
Till time its unveiled purport shew;
For many a tender thought concealed,
Just ere its object is revealed,
To disappointment's blight must yield,
And droop and die!

But lo! a new desire of mine
The present moment shall confine,
And shield it so it ne'er decline:
It is, that pleasure pure and true
May beam to-night in brightest hue;
This little thought I give to you,
Ere it can fly.

We've disappointments quite a host;
Our harvest hopes are few at most,
For well-nigh all are dead or lost.
Then let the present moment be
Filled to the brim with sinless glee;
This our joint thought to night shall be—
A happier one!

HAVING ONE TO SHARE IT.

METHINKS life's threatening cloud of ill
A fringe of light will wear it,
If we have one beside us still,
In patient love to share it.
Our very joys account we less,
The moment we compare them
With that supremer happiness
Of having one to share them!

I grasped earth's sweets in that lone hour
With selfish aim, while care—it
Came with an overwhelming power,
For I had none to share it!
But now life's griefs have mixed alloys—
Her burdens, I can bear them—
More truly estimate her joys,
For I have one to share them.

MUTUAL TEARS.

Mutual tears in union flowing—
Grief's dear gems, but shed to prove
How two hearts are closer growing
In the bonds of mutual love!
All love's cold of morn, ascending,
Changed to sorrow's sacred dew;
And the bitter trouble ending,
It shall flash in joy's fair hue.
Love shall shine out purer, sweeter,
When her dimmed horizon clears;
Pour then heavier, fall then fleeter,
Hallowed floods of mutual tears!

Only just the sore upweeding
All that might love's flowers destroy;
Only just the needful bleeding,
Forcing out the heart's alloy.
Painful wounds! yet, there escaping,
All love's refuse disappears,
For to closer union shaping
Loving hearts—those mutual tears!

Love shall shine out purer, sweeter,
When her dimmed horizon clears;
Pour then heavier, fall then fleeter,
Hallowed floods of mutual tears!

O my heart! lie still, and suffer
All that clogs thy love to go;
Be thy training harsher, rougher,
If the rank weeds stronger grow.
Pierce my heart, ye pangs of sorrow!
Search it as a thousand spears!
If but purer joy to-morrow
Flash to gems those mutual tears!
Love shall shine out purer, sweeter,
When her dimmed horizon clears;
Pour then heavier, fall then fleeter,
Hallowed floods of mutual tears!

If, these needed grief-hours over,
All that soiled be washed away,
Then the bow of hope shall hover,
Happy pledge of clearer day!
Calm I'll look, then—not with sorrow—
From the light of sunnier years,
See all gilded by that morrow,
These cold doubts and pains and fears.
Love shall shine forth brighter, sweeter,
When her dimmed horizon clears;
Pour then heavier, fall then fleeter,
Hallowed floods of mutual tears!

True love-quarrels come in blessing,
Purging out the dross, the bad;
Though awhile young hearts distressing,
In the end to make them glad.
Sent to make more kind and wise are
Such sad griefs, as each heart nears
Brighter hours, for sunnier skies are
Scanned through mist of mutual tears.
So love shines out brighter, sweeter,
When her dimmed horizon clears;
Pour then heavier, fall then fleeter,
Hallowed floods of mutual tears!

HAPPY IN THY LOVE.

Oh say'st thou that the day may come
When I shall dearer be—
When we shall share the self-same home,
And I shall dwell with thee?
And dost thou hope my future lot
May still more blissful prove?
What wish I more? for am I not
Now happy in thy love?

Thou say'st, though, that, like all earth's joy,
Not all unmixed with care—
Those draughts of bliss have much alloy,
And burdens I must bear.
No griefs shall e'er disturb my brow,
My heart shall fail to move,
If I be only then as now,
All happy in thy love!

Why should I for a future sigh
That never may be mine?
Does Nature wish her harvest nigh,
While spring-green bowers entwine?
Can future prospects charm me, when
To-day so sweet can prove?
All one to me, if now, and then,
I'm happy in thy love.

MISCELLANEOUS POEMS.

Section III.

OUR FIRST SPRING STROLL.

GOOD FRIDAY, 1860.

"Good Friday yesterday—the first spring day which has broken the monotony of one of our longest winters."—*Times, April* 7, 1860.

The mist hung motionless on meadow-slopes,
And nature breathless hailed returning spring;
The zephyr-breeze, scarce flutt'ring, fanned her hopes,
Yet no chill north-wind fears distrustful fling;
And all the shades are ambered with the light,
And hazy air is streaked with sunset red,
When round those hill-tops, balmy, soft, and bright,
Sweet spring remains, though her first day has fled.

Yet keep we glad remembrance of the hours
That first stole on that vanquished winter track,
Ere nature weaved her coronet of flowers,
And, robed in state, received her spring time back.

Within the human heart let joy's sun shine,
And sorrow's ice-wind melt in pleasure's ray;
Soon fragrant flowers of mirth spring up, entwine,
And bloom as quickly as they fade away.

Then count we now their transient petals sweet,
And store the soul's blithe incense while we may—
Tell why our hearts shared nature's bliss, and beat
With sinless pleasure on this first spring day.
Aye, more than nature's bliss! for nature's Lord
We view, our Victor, come with spoils for man,
And feel Who could such priceless gifts accord,
Would have His children joy whene'er they can.

For has not sin's dark winter passed away?
And though not yet celestial noontide blaze,
His Church rejoices in spring's genial ray,
And calmly waits her cloudless summer days.
And if at times shall Calvary's gloom return,
And fearful troubled souls in sorrow steep,
May not that Presence cause their hearts to burn,
Who see their Lord beside them as they weep?

Or courting nature's haunts, where earth's brief spring
Flits o'er the meadows in her fresh young glow,
She who once sorrowed with her suffering King,
May gaily cheer his drooping children now.
And there's no spreading landscape soft and fair,
No gentle green slope in the distance dim,
But He in spirit is most truly there,
And his own people can commune with Him.

Methinks not lacking musings such as these—
Meet meditations for this sacred day—
We too strolled out among the meads and trees,
From close and crowded city haunts away;
From Islington, once high on rural shore,
Now covered o'er by that vast heaving sea
Of human mind, nor famed as once of yore
For merry country life 'twas wont to be.

But northward, where yet rise those verdant heights
Within whose calm embrace, in peaceful glen,
Lies Hornsey's village—prettiest, best of sites
To shield her from the encroaching haunts of men!
There where the hill-slope ends, we gaily strolled,
While the young sun nor glared, but softly shone;
All o'er the land a golden mist he rolled,
Where the tired winds had left the trees alone.

By stately firs, sweet nature's green-robed towers;
By silvery stream, yon city's healthful freight;
By rural homes amid their budding bowers;
By red-tiled factory, and by white-barred gate;
From stiff and formal art we turn our eyes
O'er nature's graceful curves of shelving green;
Or to the vale, where low the river lies,
Bright in its windings to enrich the scene.

And now adown the gentle slope beyond,
Calm in the vale the first young town lies low—
Like lazy willow pool or stagnant pond,
Compared to where yon boisterous billows flow—

There, where a thousand spires, like rocks upriven,
Gaze on that human sea what storms assail!—
Here, where the plain but modest tower has given
To Heaven the simple worship of the vale.

And yet, O Enfield! not for such sweet charms,
But harsher thoughts 'tis makes thy name renowned;
When o'er the land has spread war's rude alarms,
The haughtier products of thy haunts are found.
Seems it not strange where all lies calm and still
Should sound the clang of arms, whose strokes of woe
Might roaring flash o'er valley, plain, and hill,
Stain the green sward with human blood?—yet no!

'Tis but to cherish peace, not foster war,
Armed with thy weapon, Britons keep the line,
The rocky wall, within which nestling are
A thousand dells we guard, as dear as thine!
And sloping corn-fields trembling with the breeze,
Vast peopled plains where city-sounds ascend,
And myriad bowers of tall entwining trees,
'Neath whose calm shades the winding rivers wend.

Oh may dear Albion's sylvan flower-girt lanes
Ne'er know the tramp of hostile troops, the roar
Of rifled-cannon! may melodious strains
Of maiden voices through their still nooks soar!
But the sun sinks, and yellow studded stars
All sparkling, sprinkle heaven's untraversed dome.

Why should we fill our hearts with thoughts of war,
When to our eyes such peaceful tokens come?

Oh may such quiet song-strains never cease,
But peace through Albion's isle preserve her sway!
Our evening prayer to Him, the Prince of Peace
Who died for man upon this closing day.

LOVE'S GROWTH.

I first see one I'm predisposed to love,
Should circumstances place us much together;
But time alone, by unveiled facts, can prove
If I can really do so — shew me whether
My choice is good — of course 'tis mine the power
To choose where'er I please, whate'er attraction
May charm me most—perchance her face commands
My interest, or her gentle ways and actions.

One is she of those gentle winning creatures
The heart so longs for, and so leaps to adore—
Or is that soft expression, those fair features,
What I admire, or have admired before?

But be I e'er mistaken—on reflection
Deem that, my choice, erroneous—there's no law
(If there has been no blending of affection)
Why I should not this half-framed love withdraw.
But if through intercourse grown daily dearer,
A thousand winning ways weaved round my heart,
Then sure the fruitage-time of love is nearer,
Though yet the blossoms are but out in part.

A flood of tender thoughts at early waking—
The myriad longings in the lone mid-day—
Those flashing hopes at eventide forsaking—
All brief and fickle as her transient ray—
One foreground form in nature's landscape ever,
Whate'er her shades, or by what joy-tints lit—
This is love's first phase, anxious—hopeful never;
These are the precious links to strengthen it.

Then comes the blissful hour of sweet receiving,
Freighted with silent stroll by sea or grove;
That blest companionship, so surely weaving
Fresh links for the unfinished chain of love!
And marriage is but just the affixed stamp—shewing
That truly gold, as so it was before;
For still the hallowed fetters shall be growing,
Till human power can add, can grasp no more!

That little seed was nothing till time's raining;
Those first young blossoms could not fruitage be;

The future's fertile soil and careful training,
These made the verdant, heavenward-climbing tree.
But if the once green plant be dead, decaying,
Take from the sapless trunk the grafted bough,
Upon some fresh tree twine it; there no saying,
It may re-bloom, tho' sorely drooping now.

WOMAN.

YEA, Woman! nothing more and nothing less;
Great in herself, else lacking all true greatness.
There are some women of the present day,
Are filled with an unnatural coveting
Of man's estate; who ape his thoughts and feelings,
And wish his work—disquiet, discontented,
They feed the current of their self-esteem,
Till it o'ertops the woman's loftier nature,
Drowns all her gentler and her truer feelings,
And but itself remains, like watery waste.
Such women are not what they would be; hence
They grow what they would not be—ever sighing
How they are lower than men in being women!
Ashamed of, eager to escape their nature.
These cannot see how both have their true spheres,
Yet each is incomplete without the other.

God did not give for man's companionship
A brother man, but out the dust of earth—
That part from man out-taken—made He Woman.
The air we breathe, of differing elements
Combined, becomes a unity of life.
Now if one element had been the other—
If nitrogen became the oxygen—
Where were the air, the source of life and breath?
What care which separate is accounted greater?
Each in its divers uses needs the other.
Look at the sweet diversities of nature:
Blended in beauty's vast harmonious whole,
Her undulating surface, hills and vales.
So is the wide-spread world of humankind;
Men are the hills, and women are the valleys.
Nay, scorn it not, nor blush with wounded pride!
'Tis no ungracious mean comparison.
Are men not hills, that pry into the world,
And pierce its outer life? while womankind
Like valleys nestle best in sanctity
Of their own homes, like vales girt round with hills;
So is not man their guardian? Do the vales
Say to the hills, "We have no need of you?"
Were all the valleys reared unto the hills,
Where were the hills? Did all the heights go nestle
Amid the dells, where would the valleys be?
Make all the valleys hills; unbroken plain,
Unvarying, and unlovely earth appears!
Change all the hills to valleys, and the vales
Would be —— what? Just the same on lower level.

Lower? Aye! well; we do not quite say that.
The brightening sun that kissed those upraised ridges,
And changed awhile their white wool garb to amber—
The sky o'ercharging yon proud mountain peaks—
Have dropped below the dell; so who shall say
Where are the heights of heaven, the depths of hell?
But hill and dale, mountain and valley make
Part of the charming whole of nature's beauty.
Nor then, save one is bold, the other fruitful.
All things are atoms now of one vast whole,
Veiled in the lap of future perfectness;
And things that blend, as nature's science shows us,
Are those that have their divers properties.
You run your small white fingers o'er the keys,
To charm us by your gentle harmony:
Where were the melodies if all were bass?
We are the human bass, and you the treble.
Where were the depth and graver force of ours,
Without your clearer, sweeter softness too?
We only became bass by your existence;
Alas! that we should add with too much truth
And base as well!—while you prove trebly dear,
In being treble; and the two, placed rightly,
United make the music of the world;
The virtue and the unselfishness of earth,
All its endearing charms and peaceful joys,
Its nearness and its progress to the future,
These are the blendings of the sundered atoms.
And better far one fragment of that whole,

Though framed of lesser fragmentary pieces,
Than one huge unit rounded to itself.
For all on earth must be disjointed fragments.
Yea, all things here are stamped with incompleteness.
In art, in fields of science unexplored,
In man, in morals, all are strewn asunder,
Like crumbled fabrics, half-built edifices,
And the great end, to "fitly frame together."
The present is the future's architect,
Mankind the builders; 'tis the only structure
With base on earth and pinnacles in heaven.
But part must fit with part: for every portion
Has its allotted place; each single truth is
Part of the puzzle to be reconstructed,
While we, but children, are but half in earnest,
Content to play with and to spoil the pieces.
But lo! the building shall arise, the puzzle
Be put together, every atom blended!
And Love 's the magnet-force of gravity
(Love, the grand principle, and not the partial
And selfish passion) that is still attracting,
Till what is just preparatory here,
There brought together in one compact mass,
And rounded into shape symmetrical,
Cemented into one grand orb of truth,
The brightness of whose glory's blaze no mortal
May gaze on here; but there, all reunited,
Still kept together by the power of Love—
The subtle gravitating force of Heaven—
Each atom shall attest its proud existence,
A needful part of the all-perfect whole!

WILD TRIBES.

Real flowers grow wild in rough and dreary places,
Where few e'er cared to stay;
And all their crude and half-developed graces
Decked but the lone highway—
Till one came there, and took the plant neglected
To his own cultured bowers,
And soon its charms and hidden worth detected,
And reared its ripening powers.
And so ere long the wayside flower was reckoned
(As everybody knows)
Our garden Queen, nor to her sister second—
The statelier, richer rose.

Thronged thick, uncared for in life's waste deserted
The wild of mortal kind!
Till for their good some noble minds concerted
Their long-veiled worth to find;
Who brought them out and gave them prouder duties
To nerve the awakened will—
Fresh hopes, fresh aims, fresh aspirations, new ties,
New achievements to fulfil:
And now the violet-mind of lowliest station
May pass that threshold by;

Wealth, valor, wisdom know no elevation
But it can soar as high.
Thanks be to those, then, whose the occupation
The untutored ones to inspire—
To illume the lowliest by-ways of our nation
With learning's hallowed fire—
To grope 'mid poverty's dark shades distressing,
Bind up want's wounds that bleed—
Thanks for their aims! be theirs the patriot's blessing!
Oh, may their work succeed,
Till through the night of misery, want, and sorrowing,
A brighter dawn shall shine,
And mortal flowers from each their fragrance borrowing,
In sweetest union twine!

THE OPENING OF THE CHURCH AND LITERARY UNION, ISLINGTON.

NOVEMBER, 1861.

Slowly the year is emptying its last stores
Of human actions and of life's events,
Into the vast unfathomable well
Where they lie silently, though not less safe,
'Till they gush forth again in myriad channels,
To scare or gladden mortal gazers on them.
What peals are knelling out the passing year?
Do the joy-bells of hope and love and peace,
Resounding sweetly through the universe,
Inspire all hearts and brighten every home?
Shall the loud Christmas anthem—soon to swell
In every Christian temple of our land,
Soaring to heaven amid earth's glad embrace—
Shall its glad tidings of a peace and joy
Won by celestial love for fall'n mankind,
Shall it find echo in all earthly hearts,
While love and peace hold universal sway?
Alas, alas! I catch discordant sounds,
Dull knells of sorrow 'mid those peals of joy.
I hear the tread of armies, and the roar
Of dire artillery, and the anguished wail

Of orphaned children, and the dying groans
Of wounded mortals by their own kin slain.
I see the despot with his iron rein
Curbing a nation into slothful ease;
And progress lying scathed at tyrants' feet.
I see, too, others lashed to furious speed,
And thousands goaded with the spurs of folly
To miscall anarchy and sad misrule
And hasty counsels of misguided men
Unlearned, by sacred name of Liberty.
Aye, e'en in land of light, where Freedom's torch
And Truth's bright lamps blaze goodly beacon-fires
I see the flickering shadows, dusky hues
And mists of ignorance, scarcely to be pierced,
And clouds of crime, so slow to clear away!
And in the halls of Truth itself—the arenas
Of science, of religion, and philanthropy—
I note the petty clamorings of pride,
The vain disputings of the haughty tongue,
Which Love herself, with all her gentle arts,
Essays in vain to quell. Oh! sad indeed
Such sights, such sounds! well may the muffled bell
Toll out in solemn dirge the wasted year!
Though better far that peals of hope should clang
With holier wishes for the year untried,
From those who, turning, gaze on brighter pictures.
I see—O goodly sight!—a nation great
Gather its strength for peace, and call to battle,
Not with the trumpet-note to bloody field,
But in the busy town, a goodly host

Of peaceful advocates of art and science.
To battle, did I say? to friendly combat,
And noble rivalry in arts of peace
With every nation; not to lash each other,
But to unite, to elevate, improve
Their fellow men of every clime and tongue.
Well may those noble domes and myriad spires
Rise unabashed to glare in heaven's pure sunshine.
But, O my country! not thy well-earned conquests,
Thy untold wealth, thy stores of knowledge famed,
Thy unmatched commerce, and above them all
Thy laws and institutions just and free—
Not these thy glory! rather this thy boast,
That thou art loth to draw again thy sword,
E'en though thy trampled honor claim redress;
That thou hast borne the taunts of envious foes,
The insults of thy thankless heritage;
Conscious of right and overwhelming force,
Canst yet refrain to strike, or rise regretful,
To mete out chastisement well merited
Upon a sister-land. Example great!
Spread far and wide, as this our time attests
How slowly nations now arise to battle!
Not with the barbarous frequency of yore,
For lust of power, or territorial gain,
Or kingly aggrandizement, to plunge two lands
In bloody contest terribly severe,
But of such rare occurrence, wars assume
A mighty import; struggles long and fierce
Now only waged, thank Heaven! for principle.

And surely now we stand upon the threshold
Of such a time of strife, the last and fiercest,
Such as this world has never groaned beneath!
Two diverse elements are gathering strength
For final contest—vice, oppression, here,
With anarchy and tyranny combined,
And all the blackness of the slavish mind,
'Gainst truth, enlightenment, and liberty.—
Which side are we, the future of our land,
Destined perchance to garner good or ill,
To enrich a coming age with this one's reapings—
Are we prepared to gird our mental powers,
To search out truth, such truth as makes us free,
Not fetters us with forms of little import,
Nor binds us slaves to narrow bigotry?
We must dive deep into Truth's holy well,
Not stand to dabble with the surface-waters,
Wasting our time in fruitless arguments,
And petty bickerings of party strife.
Not such our aim who, meeting thus to-night,
Would consecrate our efforts and our time
To prove Religion does not disavow
Nor seek to ignore the intellectual powers,
But throws her halo round all earthly studies;
To prove Religion does not wear a mask
Of dark misanthropy, but weaves a charm
O'er cheerful social fellowship, and converse
Of youthful minds for study and for pleasure.
This be our task, and this the arena for it!
Sharpened our intellect, well-stored our mind,

By friendly converse and by mutual study,
So shall we take our place in manhood's rank,
For sterner conflict, and for higher duties:
To cope with error, and to trample vice,
Side with the good, and to assist the free.
And if our lot in actual war to mingle,
Be ours the cause of right and peace and freedom,
To guard our land, secure tranquillity,
And waft its blessings e'en to foreign shores.
Be ours to feel then, that our youthful converse
And mutual study have not been for nought—
That we, companions now, may rank together
In that great conflict in the cause of truth:
Our ever-cherished object, then as now,
The union of our own pure faith with knowledge.

VEILED.

The kernel, fashioned in the spring,
Was hung amid the leaves—
But now the shell, a coarser thing,
All time and care receives.

The gem was hoarded years before—
Time now, when all the aim
Seems, to forget, to shroud it o'er,
The casket rich to frame!

Let them alone; if underneath
The fruit be ripening still—
If flashing through, though half in stealth,
The gem that void shall fill.

Let them alone; there comes the day
Thrown off the shell shall fall,
Unthought of, prized not, cast away—
The fruit found all in all!

Let them alone; these caskets fade;
To prize them who'll endeavor?
The jewel on her heart is laid
For ever and for ever.

UNTHREADED.

WEAVE thee a girdle for thy love to wear,
And clasp around her with a silver clasp;
Silks of the finest qualities combined,
Rich colours of the rainbow interwoven,
And threads of varied hues together blended,
In a harmonious, perfect, graceful whole,
Pure and befitting ornament to grace
A maiden queen — no gaudy tints prevailing;
All softened to a tasteful, chaste design,
Meet circlet to adorn a virgin waist.

Fashioned the girdle! of the choicest hues,
Richest material, costly, elegant—
But lacking — so 'twas thought — the simple charm
Of sober neatness and unsullied grace.
One color seemed to assert a sovereign sway,
Outshining all the rest—imperial hue,
Too proud to mingle in a circlet meek
Of quiet colors, sweetly grouped to clasp
A gentle maiden in their bright embrace.
Unthread the work! go, fashion it afresh;
Take the same tints, but see not one prevail
Above the others; with more wisdom blend them.

Dispute not, question not the undoubted failure;
Weep not, e'en if the work of years be wasted,
But recommence, work with redoubled zeal:
So shall experience crown success at last.

It was a band of love I would have clasped
Around my dear one's heart! I fashioned it
From an idea that years had conjured up;
Methought it were the best I could bestow,
The richest, brightest, loveliest ornament
'Twas mine to offer! I would cast it round her!

Let me be brave—with failure so apparent,
Most idle, cowardly, to dispute, deny it—
Let me be brave! my soul, is it not certain
So much undue predominance exists
Of one part over every other portion,
That so it lacks the best embellishment,
That has no flaunting, no unseemly parts
Offensive in the slightest form to taste,
But simple, chaste, unglaring ornament,
Meet for a virgin heart? Be firm, my soul!
Unthread it, though the dear design of years
Become of nothing worth—my heart, be cheered!
Retain the same hues—after the same kind
Remodel it—thou dost not lack material;
But be each part a check upon the other,
Each tint to soften each; no arrogance
Of unveiled hue protruding in relief,
Flaming the girdle with its pride of power;

For lowliness of purpose and design,
With nought of violence, but quiet strength,
Shall best accord with gentle maidenhood.
Bring thou the qualities that make thy love—
Once like young children, fully grown to vigor
Wreathed to one purpose in their union firm—
Slowly unthread the last; and yet more slowly
Entwine the old threads after wiser fashion.
Be not dismayed, my soul, undone, impatient!
Be humble, teachable, yet firm and hopeful;
And thou shalt yet weave for thy love a girdle
Of such sweet tints, in such admired proportion,
That she shall proudly wear it round her heart.

Weave we life's girdle e'er with wrong material?
Often! and ever in undue proportions!
Part of one piece, we know, the work is wasted;
Life's threads can never be unthreaded. Never?
Thank Heaven that varied are our life's achievements!
Each separate work may have refashioning.
Is it ambition, sordid, proud, tyrannic?
'Tis harmonized to noble emulation;
Or pride, unlovely, harsh, disdainful, chilling?
'Tis moulded to unblemished dignity;
Mere earthly passion, selfish and unholy,
Changed to youth's virgin, undefiling love.

With patience and humility, yet firmly,
Let us unthread the unmeet, glaring, gaudy;
And be our life an ever fresh refashioning.

So we possess the meetest ornaments
That God requires, here fashioned in earth's work-
room,
There clasped around His robe of righteousness.

SUMMER.

The sun returned, and on the flashing waves
Shed forth his genial glow; and all the air
Rushed from the south with still increasing warmth,
And rested on the waters; and the tides
Bore them yet onward to the island shore,
Where broke the billows into thousand gems
Weaved by meridian sunlight; while sea-breezes
Bounded o'er tall white cliffs, and kissed the meadows,
And ambered them with flowers; and all the grass
Waved greenly with its glad acknowledgment;
And little dells drank down the balmier air;
And patient waiting hills caught up the gales,
And flung them to the plains and through the forest;
While fresh green woods enshrined the subtle power,
Hid it 'neath leafy screens, where spreading boughs
Met and embraced for very joyousness.

And scattered farms awoke to rural life,
And cheerful homesteads peeped through floral bowers;
E'en crowded haunts caught somewhat of the sunshine,
And man himself, elated by its influence,
Rejoiced, and into imaged queen of beauty
Personified this power, and crowned her Summer.
But Nature was the manager of all,
The chief prime mover at the festival.
She had lain sleeping when the voice of mirth
Rang out from lighted town, where revels gay
Flashed in the dazzling halls at eventide,
Where Pleasure, from her palaces within,
Recked not the desolation rife without.
Yea, e'en the merriment aroused her not,
That grouped around the fireside's cheering glow;
Nor where in well-warmed rooms the merry strains
Of gentle voices pierced the winter gloom;
She slumbered on, unmindful of it all,
And sighed upon the wind that blurred the street-lights,
Or moaned in blasts that shook the fastened doors.
But now she awakes to glee, and summons back
From the soft south her feathered choristers;
Retunes her harp, prepares her festal strains—
And all her harmony bursts forth anew:
The leaflet's rustling, and the stream's gay ripple,
The plashing of the brooks and waterfalls,
The sky-lark's merry trill, the gentler note

Of woodland thrush and modest nightingale,
The buzz of insects, hum of active bees—
Yea, heedless man—unmindful of her griefs—
She bids renew his strains, nor silent rest,
But with a cheerful and a blithesome spirit,
With flowers and insects, birds and bees and rivers,
Join in her newly awakened songs of joy,
In laughing groups upon the hill-tops gathering,
Prolonging in her moonlight groves the revels;
Nor wanting, too, the music of the heart,
The inner incense of each vocal lay.
May no rough blasts break in upon her glee,
Nor mar her merriment! no chilling rains
Damp her delights! no pall-white cloud o'ershadow
Her many charms! but cheerful sunlight fall
With brilliant hues upon her countless beauties!
But chiefly may all troublous storms depart,
And sorrow's darksome hours and chilling rains!
May cheerful sunlight rest upon the hearts
Of that unnumbered throng of happy beings
She bids become her human choristers!

SUMMER RAINS.

SUMMER visions, clear and pleasant!
Sunny skies and balmy air!
All the sweets of nature present,
Gay green boughs and flow'rets fair.
Summer fancies! never shrouded
By the noon-day tempest's ire!
Summer fancies, all unclouded!
While no chilling wet eves tire.

Summer truths! how oft the languor
Of the sun's unyielding glare
Dulls its lustre, till in anger
Nature draws her cloud-veils there!
Then the poured-forth rain-drops banish
Burning moments, cool the air;
And the threatening cloud-forts vanish,
And the chastened rays shine there.

Fall, ye summer rain-drops! lightly
On our fevered hearts to lie,
When joy's sunbeams glare too brightly,
And the tempering breezes die.

E'en life's summers have their sorrows;
Nature's yield their genial rain;
May they both bring clear to-morrows,
Freshened to new life again!

SUMMER INCENSE.

Silently stealing along on the breezes,
Unseen yet unstayed in its love-mission fleet,
Away o'er fair spots where each nature-charm pleases,
To the filth of close alleys, the din of the street;

Uprising from where the mown grass-heaps are
lying
So calmly, on fresh breezy hill-tops at rest,
To where, oh, sad contrast! poor torn hearts are
sighing,
By the eager gold seekers so jostled and prest!

From the rustling and rippling and chirping sounds,
telling
How nature's blithe accents are happy and free,
To where, from their secret depths, earth-griefs
outwelling,
Show, save with man only, work pleasant can be.

The man grasping wealth townward eagerly hurries,
Nor heeds the cool breath of the morn on his brow;
For some dim golden future, the cares and the worries
Of close city-life are his heart's idols now.

Yet, sweet scent of hay-fields! awhile with us tarry!
Some hearts wait the pleasure thy presence can yield;
Our thoughts from town-cares to the quiet nooks carry,
Where One has so scented the grass of the field!

Through the harsh dreary winter, by chilling snows shrouded,
Grow the young grass-blades by meadow and lea,
While recked not by man in his city-haunt crowded,
Treasure they silently sweet stores of thee!

ON THE THRESHOLD.

Come to the threshold, dearest! where entranced—
Without, all cold, within, all brilliancy—
We paused, and viewed the arena of delights,
And fair array of bright and festal scenes,
Long rows of lighted hours all spread before us,
Ere hand in hand, with buoyant hearts elated,
We wandered forth together in their midst.
If e'er the midst shall tell a tale of tiring,
Of cups of bliss drained off too greedily,
Palling because too sweet—as ball-room guests,
Whom close and crowded rooms of glare and light
Shall tire and weary, urging them to seek
The cooler area of the entrance way—
So be it then with us—if valuing less,
Or viewing with less clear and happy eyes
Our fuller present, let us back again,
To stand within the threshold—not to cross it,
But only where the cold and gloom without
Remind us of the warmth and comfort here—
To view the scene as first all glad we viewed it,
Its joys to appreciate rightly, as of yore,
Our bliss comparing with its distant lustre—
Come, maiden! to the threshold.

Is it lowering
A holy love, to liken it to pleasure,
To city scenes of evening gaiety?
Is it the rather some sweet landscape, where
These blest in daylight wander?—Be it so.
Back to that boundary hill, then, where we met,
And gazed transported on the scene beneath us,
Then joining company to share its beauties.
If thorny tracts, rough, rocky steeps fatigue,
Or stream-mists damp, or heights obscure the prospect,
Or noontide veil it in less lovely hue—
Back to that boundary hill! that, as of yore,
We view the rich and wide-spread landscape round us;
That so we learn, who've roamed amid its scenes,
How rough rock steeps, and thorny tangled paths,
And meadows damped with many impeding streams,
And bare heights blotting out the distant view—
Things in themselves that vex and tire and pain—
Yet tend each one to grace the wide survey,
Fill up the varied whole with finished beauty!

Alas! but we can backward pass no more,
To gaze as thus we gazed upon the threshold!
Love's first blithe entrance-way is closed for ever;
We must go onward towards two exits grim—
Both of them sad, but one by far the saddest—
Or death, or cruel separation; so
True axiom this: light's end must needs be darkness;

And love, the whitest square in all our lives,
Must have its limit somewhere in the shade-hues!
Only like black rock, channelled, broken through,
Where love's stream, hid, runs on to heavenly
springs.

Aye, but we may in thought returning thither,
Catch somewhat of the freshness of that time,
And view the scene (if truly viewed aright
By love's first glance) as spread then rich around
us,
And knowing how those sterner parts forbidding
Are all accessories needful to the picture,
E'en as we reach them one by one, resolved
To face them and to pass them manfully,
Assured these ills may atoms prove of good,
So from fond memory's pleasant halting place
Go forward on our mutual way rejoicing!

Joy at the outset may appear the brightest,
Just as the first draught oft shall taste most sweet;
At each life-banquet we commence to eat
With keener relish, for the heart is lightest—
Then to the threshold, maiden, come with me!

If years should pale, or time should tire our joy,
Disputes e'er chill it with their icy breath,
Or clouds of sorrow hide it underneath,
If, drained too oft, the cup of bliss should cloy—
Come to the threshold, maiden, come with me!

Come to the threshold, when our fainting hearts
Grow fevered in the atmosphere of pleasure;
Or count it less, oblivious of the measure;
To view our joy complete in all its parts,
Come to the threshold, maiden, come with me!

Come to the hill-top, where love's fresh morn found us,
If e'er the rocks should tire, or thorns should tear,
If e'er the way a less sweet aspect wear—
To view the prospect richly spread around us,
Come to the threshold, maiden, come with me!

To learn that joy its atoms has of sorrow—
Component parts, each needful to the whole,
The perfect integral—so this console;
That all prepared we face love's fickle morrow—
Come to the threshold, maiden, come with me!

We may not seek it as before we sought;
We 've but two exits, death or separation;
We ne'er shall stand again at that old station.
Aye, but we may return again in thought!
Come to the threshold, maiden, come with me!

If e'er our love should droop as though 't would die,
If years e'er dim it, bring satiety—
In keeping holy anniversary,
We'll to the threshold, dearest! you and I—
Come to the threshold, maiden, come with me!

A YEAR'S GARNERINGS.

HIS first spring charms long faded,
In Autumn's bronze hues jaded,
By Winter's cold gloom shaded—
So dies our once young year!
He has stolen how many a token!
What fragment-joys now broken!
What fond words now ne'er spoken!
Yet much he leaves us here.

Calm the new year expecting,
Let 's forth, fresh flowers collecting
(Each weed of ill rejecting),
Lodged in the old year's soil.
These with a thousand new seeds—
Let 's hope with still more few weeds—
Products of good and true deeds,
Plant in the new year's soil.

What though oft sown in weeping,
'Neath earth a long time keeping,
Nor quick in blossom leaping,
Those fruits of all our toil—
Each year shall add its treasure,
A richer, fuller measure;
Pain yet shall leave its pleasure—
Success's fragrant oil!

LINES COMPOSED FOR AN ALBUM.

Poësy's Grave.

What use the heart's untrammelled thrill?
What use the freshly wakened lay?
Bury those strains that are fit but to fill
The void of an age past away!
This present of fact and action plain,
And rapid thought, and busy brain,
What room for the quiet and gentle strain?
Where may the minstrel's song be laid?
Anywhere, in the unnoticed shade,
Away from an age that will but scorn—
Till Poësy's night of neglect shall fade,
And her new and holier æra dawn.

'Mid the many-colored leaves,
Where the autumn tints are strewn,
Cast the unregarded sheaves
That a callous world disown.
Swiftly fleet the chilling eves—
Patience! comes the summer day;
And the heart's true poetry leaves
Harvest stores, that still shall stay.

So within this little book
Proudly these few lines I lay,
Where the fair ones deign to look,
'Mid its varied leaves so gay—
Vernal green to wintry red—
This at least the muse's shrine;
Here (unto a harsh world dead)
May her lighter fancies shine.
In the home-throng with the fair,
Wait thee, Muse! more prosperous days;
Thine an honored burial there—
Rest ye still, my little lays!

THE OPENING OF THE METROPOLITAN RAILWAY.

The deep mud pool in the meadow lies,
And sunders the carpet of shining green;
And the rural beauty and freshness dies
In the dense town-gulf that yawns between.
The messenger fleet from the valleys sweet
Halts on the edge, with its freight of lives;

To the nest of lanes and the swaying street
From on either side its load it gives —
Some who ne'er go back to the quiet track,
Where the birds trill softly, and streamlets plash
past,
Whom the rural shore shall for ever lack,
Held in the depths of that town-gulf fast!
A sea of gold, running gaily and fair,
This mass of city to some may seem,
With nothing to soil the myriads there,
As they pass and repass in that heaving stream —
So, sundering thousands from rural charms,
Wedging them in 'mid its murky ways,
It casts round about them its tight-clasped arms,
And its captives lie bound there their life-long days.

On the slimy pool the bridge is hung,
And the banks of green are sundered no more!
And the messenger passes the streets among;
Unstayed, he speedeth from shore to shore.
And the iron band from the quiet land
Is cleaving the adamant mass in twain,
Till no more alone and defiant it stand,
But the two have been moulded to peace again.

O highway, linking those sundered ways!
Thou first young sign of a future to be —
Dawning of brighter and better days!
Thou bringest a vision all fair to me:

I see a city, not cramped in space,
Nor wrapped in an isolation single,
Where the town-throng no more the still haunts
displace,
But both in a wondrous union mingle.
I see the lone crest of the verdant hills,
Where the spreading trees to the breezes sway;
In the valleys I hear the murmur of rills,
While the slopes are decked with the dwellings gay.
And no longer in solid bulk extend
The close-packed haunts, while the green meads flee;
But both in a scene of beauty blend,
The thronged highways with the woodland free.
And the wide streets like gold bands stretch away
O'er the wood-clothed hills, through the rural vales;
And the country is wedded to town-haunts gay
By the magic spell of the iron rails.

O wondrous Steam! thou hast yet but run
A tithe of thy race to that future goal;
Thy prosperous work, so well begun,
Go forth and speed to the perfect whole!

SUCCESS.

COMPOSED ON THE OCCASION OF A CONVERSAZIONE OF THE CHURCH AND LITERARY UNION, ISLINGTON.

Last night I mused upon our meeting here—
Its aim, and what might make it prove successful.
Success! strange thing of varied shape and hue;
A bright-plumed bird, that now on rapid wing,
E'en while we know it not, has flown to meet us.
Now like a distant, sunlit, silver sea
In tidal flow, advancing while retreating,
Slowly it climbs the strand to kiss our feet.
The bold idea amid the battle's travail—
A gleam of bayonets and a flash of sabres,
A sudden charge, a shout prolonged, triumphant—
And lo! the fight is o'er, the victory won!
A flash of thought that quick illumes a mind,
Big with its use, or brimmed with wondrous beauty—
And lo! amid its light, Success is seen!
A fairy fabric with its halls of beauty,
And gleaming domes, and marble walls and columns.
But oftener, like earth's monuments substantial,
We rear it slowly up through pain and failure—

A brick or two each weary aching day,
Till time has capped it with its bright gold turrets.

But soon my thoughts, grown vague, confused, and dim,
In kind the same, ran on through mist of sleep;
And on a wide-spread plain with crowd of towers,
And blocks of buildings pierced by noble highways,
The stately city to completion grew.
The work went on, wrought silently, but surely;
Unstayed by opposition thick and fierce
Of factious multitudes from neighbouring towns,
Who would not if they could perceive its use,
Or own its beauty — but the work is wrought.
Surely Success is there? that opening day,
I see pour through its streets a mighty train,
Throng in its temples, fill its myriad marts;
Forests of upreared banners, festal music,
Gay vessels, hung with flags, and filled with men,
Glide blithely on its sunny river's breast.
And lo! they come from many a league around,
From neighboring towns, from hamlets far away —
The glad abettors, or the opposers silenced —
And swell the grandeur of the inauguration.
But time is bribed not 'mid that pomp to stay;
The sun sinks down upon that proud rejoicing —
Days come and go, suns smile upon the city —
On purposes achieved? on ripe success?
Alas, alas! frost nips the young spring bud!

I see the city, proud and stately still,
Wrapt by the sunlight in a silent beauty.
Its domes and pinnacles are glowing fair,
Its waters flash—but all is *silent* charm
And one black cloud, one mantle of dark night
May show chill scene of empty desolation!
One thing alone was wanting—as dead form,
So fair and perfect still, that needs alone
The warm blood to gush through its thousand veins—
For lack of the life-throng, the city lies
A dead and silent thing; and the rank grass
Grows up, where late that happy crowd swept on;
And its yet new and gorgeous buildings—shells!
Mere empty ones, that boast no harvest stores;
The multitudes have gone to other scenes,
Have left the city to decay again.
Thus slowly reared the temple of Success
By patient labor, efforts laudable,
As the proud wave-crest in its transient whiteness
Lifts its tall summit to fall back again.
And then methought: now will that area vast
Of noble buildings all be razed and levelled;
And broken columns, crumbled grass-strewn fragments
Attest alone an idle useless city!

But lo! an age has in my dream swept by;
And once again I see that city fair
Now flushed with life through every teeming way,
With busy streets, and noisy avenues,

And cheerful mansions, and filled halls of commerce.
Not one of all the thousand buildings there
Stands reared for nought; all have their varied uses.
And as I mused upon the wondrous change,
A whisper came to me: "If wrought the work
For noble objects, though all inauspicious
The object of our cherished care have proved,
Destroy it not. Wait! use fresh stores of patience;
And if it be a wise and noble thing,
Just like the city,—that was truly needed,
Though thousands all opposing knew it not—
Its aim shall have the future full fruition."

Now, though my dream has passed from me, I know
Success is seldom just to-day's brief pleasure,
Nor e'en the finely finished structure, reared
Through the long tedious days to perfect form:
But that shaped object still *preserved* and *cherished*
With jealous care, with anxious, endless watching;
Like glad stream ever flowing, ever widening,
That daily bubbles up from sparkling source,
An age's joy, a life's fertility!

IN THE ROOM OF.

In the old room at eventide,
When the shadows had stolen away,
And the sun shone bright in its softened light,
At the close of the summer day.

Over each familiar thing it shone
With its calm and tranquil glow;
Like a smile it 'lighted upon each one
Where had hovered the shade of woe.

It glanced on the well-used instrument—
Where her fingers had loved to stray,
Till a new harp's strains with Heaven's chorus blent,
And the earth-notes had died away! —

Like an angel it slid through the flashing pane
To the floor where her feet had trod;
Soothing the hearts that had stricken lain —
Sweet comforter sent from God! —

Gilding anew with a burnished frame
Her drawings that hung on the wall:
Thus those soft beams to that old room came,
Cheering and brightening all.

So e'en to my soul those sun-rays streamed,
Where the lone night had fled away,
And my heart once more at their greeting seemed
To leap in the light of day.

And they pierced to the inmost chamber of all,
That long had been locked and left,
That their sweet calm light once more might fall
Where the past and its memories slept.

And I tried to arouse that form again,
That joy of a past that was o'er,
That so long in my heart had silent lain —
Shall it wake? Shall it wake no more?

Face of an early youth fleeted away,
Come back in the sunshine to me!
Come as of yore in that vanished day! —
But never a form could I see.

Blossom of spring-time, broken and dead!
I would picture you as you were!—
Vain, vain! no recalling an image long fled—
I could see but one figure there.

So I closed my eyes, and I strove yet again
'Mid the past and its scenes to be;
But that joy had been sundered by gulf of pain;
'Twas the present alone I could see.

Oh! it vexed me sore I could trace no more
('Whelmed 'neath this present glee)
The form that I then so loved to adore,
That was all in all to me!

Did the noiseless rays grow vocal then,
To comfort me and reprove?
Had some angel sought out the haunts of men,
With a message of heavenly love?

Sure 'tis a voice that was hushed, I hear,
As in sunny eves vanished from me!
Sure an angel spirit hath touched my ear
(But never a form could I see)!

"Seek not to disentomb the past;
God buried it secretly;
Somewhere in the depths of thy heart 'twas cast,
Let it there unfathomed lie.

"I, too, had thoughts of the things of earth,
And of one there dear to me—
It was love, not pain, that gave them birth,
For in heaven pain could not be;

"And yet, as amid that blissful throng
I thought of an earth-hope dear,
A mournful cadence had caught my song,
And it jarred upon seraph-ear—

"And swift to heaven's holiest court there sped
A half-whispered prayer from me
(For though thou must not pray for the dead,
Yet the dead may pray for thee);

"And He spake, who once upon earth did live,
Who feels all human pain:
'A special mission to thee I give:
Go, spirit! to earth again;

"'Go, till thy strains once more rise clear,
Dimmed by no earth-note of ill;
Till then, away from this sorrowless sphere,
And work upon earth My will.'

"So I wandered forth from those realms of the blest,
To where His guidance led,
'Mid sin and sorrow to work His behest—
To find for thee one in my stead.

"So I wandered, till came there a flash of the past,
Of a face that had long passed away;
Then I knew that my wanderings were over at last,
That 'twas here my mission lay!

"A fair brow stamped with maiden truth—
Bright eyes that with love flashed clear—
One whom I felt he had guided in youth—
I knew that my mission was here.

"So I twined with thine own her thread of life,
That henceforth on thy love she might lean;
She will make thee a fond and faithful wife,
Even as I would have been

"(For I—my whole heart was set on thee then,
In one current with thine to flow,
Till He trained me to quit the haunts of men,
And bade thee let me go).

"So alike, that thy wearied and lonesome heart
Might find here its natural rest—
As the bird, from its young brood torn apart,
May have nestled in kindred nest.

"The old has been moulded afresh—re-cast,
Re-shaped in the present anew;
And thou may'st not recal that faded past,
Thou only the present shalt view.

"So unlike! two separate beings, e'en though
The first in the second be merged—
As two paths at a point blended, far sundered go,
The one from the other diverged.—

"My glad task is over, His mission is done;
I ascend back to regions of bliss:
For that old tie's sake, be ye henceforth one;
'Tis his gift—oh! forget not this.

"Leave the past to sleep on, till the trumpet-call
Shall awake it to life once more,
Till three beings low at one throne shall fall,
United His Name to adore."

Noiselessly, sweetly, the crimsoning light
In that old room fell soft and fair;
And the past it had vanished from out of my sight,
And only the present was there!

In the old room at eventide,
When the sunlight was stealing away—
But she I so cherish was by my side,
Far dearer to me than the day!

They may strive to sever our loves in twain,
With their plots by the Evil One led;
But surely such scheming shall prove in vain,
For an angel hath twined the thread!

May our joint lives, lengthened as He sees fit,
One golden thread closer grow;
Closer and closer our hearts be knit,
In a world of strife and woe!

Then meeting at heaven's porch, there three side by side,
Where earth's narrow bonds are all riven,
Ever loving (but a spark of that love of the Bride,
Whose whole love to the Bridegroom is given)—

Loving each other as others we love,
All free from earth's sin-taint and leaven,
Loving as do the bright angels above,
There, all pure, in the kingdom of heaven!

LIFE'S DRILLINGS.

"In the world's broad field of battle,
In the bivouac of life."—LONGFELLOW.

RIGHT ABOUT FACE!

HALT, halt! for the foemen lie thickly beyond ye,
And the more ye march on, they 'll the more hem
you in;
But still there's escape; courage, then! nor despond
ye;
To the right, to the right! and your way back begin.

To the right? Nay, 'twere vain; we must have no
half measures,
No tampering at all with the craft of the foe;
Ye must march quite away from these mischievous
pleasures;
To the right *about* first, then, ere forward ye go!

Indeed, ye are marching to rearward, believe me;
The true front is behind, though ye may not discern;
For the foeman hath purposely leagued to deceive
ye;
Then face the true way, to the right about turn!

Their treaties were vain, and their truce was all
hollow;
With a semblance of peace they have led on their
prey;
With their cunning beguilements they lured ye to
follow—
But while there is time, from their snares break
away!

I know that the land ye return to lies higher—
I know that the way is rough, toilsome, uphill;
That the foe will attack you the more ye retire,
And force you to fight him — but right about still!

There's a soft trait'rous balm in the air you're in-
haling;
It wooes you to sloth, and it lulls you to sleep,
And it makes you crave more for each sinful re-
galing —
But there's healthier atmosphere high on the steep.

Though for so long entrapped in the enemy's region,
Regain ye your countrymen's manners and strength!
Become ye a brave, an invincible legion,
To halt in your own native country at length.

Aye, from each fiercest fight, after each desperate
rally
Emerging, the land of your Lord ye shall trace —
View clearer each hill-slope, each soft golden valley —
Delay then no longer, but right about face!

FORWARD.

FORWARD now! success attend ye!
Never look behind;
And while life's long steep ascend ye!
Well your footing mind.

Fret not for the fading pleasures
Ye have left below;
Covet more those priceless treasures
Which to attain ye go.

Never heed the thorns that tear ye,
Though they oft may wound;
Struggle on, footsore and weary —
Gain the higher ground!

Practise every good and wise work —
This your strength shall be:
Sins of every shape and guise lurk
Near, to vanquish ye.

Yea, they still pursue you ever —
Strive to keep them back!
Let them gain the mastery never;
Faint not at the attack.

Firm your hand on duty's plough place;
Work with heart and will,
And your home, yon mountain's brow, trace —
Oh, then, forward still!

Forward! and success attend you!
See ye look not back;
And the God of heaven defend you
On your perilled track;

At its happy closing own you,
Where no foes pursue;
There in His own regions crown you
Victors brave and true!

FORM COMPANY.

NOT alone, but united, let's work while we can;
Let man meet with man in commingling array;
Let us search out and succour the destitute man,
And the ignorant and vicious improve while we may.

Let each to his regiment; the foeman is nigh!
United, not scattered, we meet him to-day;
For methinks from our disciplined forces he'll fly,
When each regiment stands ready in battle array.

Each man to his company! varied may be
And divers the duties ye have to fulfil;
But whate'er may betide him, let every man see
He stand true to his work, to his company still.

What! what! you would combat alone with the foe—
All unaided your flag of defiance unfurled!
Do you think, while no regiment, no drilled force you know,
You can go forth and vanquish the might of the world?

The foeman is coming — sin, squalor, and woe,
Want, ignorance, and vice — it is these ye must meet;
Let every man forth to his company go;
For alone and unaided must bring but defeat.

The sin-loving worldling all idle may be;
The courtier of Pleasure may fawn at her feet;
But we have our duty to do first, and we
Must be up and all ready the foeman to meet.

Let the young and the foolish, the idle and vain
Deem we are all gloomy, while they are all gay;
We've our work to be done, we've our victory to gain —
But we 're quite as light-hearted and happy as they.

'Tis the same foe we meet, the same battle we fight;
Though our tactics be varied, we seek the same ends;
Then let no man go singly. Together, unite!
The foe is at hand! — to your regiments, my friends!

HALT!

Came spring-time; o'er the drooping vales
The soft south sea-borne zephyrs drop;
While seek the harsh rude winter gales
Their last stronghold, the mountain-top.

There, girdled by their troops of snow,
The storm-fiends, raging loud and long,
Shriek, wailing forth dull notes of woe
Adown their rocky fortress strong.

A few days since, and one went by
In young life's rash unbridled zeal;
That life he gave to the cold sky,
And perished for some dim ideal!

Now dawn with her chameleon flame
Upon the valley blithely lay,
When to the mountain's foot there came
A traveller who would pass that way.

Wistful he eyed his urgent track
Across the snowy crimsoned peak;
But calm experience kept him back —
He would no futile peril seek.

He knew that hero's tragic fate —
How stealthy storms yet cowered above —
More wise, determined he to wait,
Till spring's soft glows his fears remove.

One, two, three tedious days pass by,
And many come and turn away;
But though not then the ascent he'd try,
Yet would he there in patience stay.

No loving maiden gently pressed
The way-worn traveller to stay,
Or bade him on her bosom rest,
Till the fierce storms should roll away.

But in some mean rude hostelry,
Scanty and coarse by day his fare,
Ill sheltered from the inclement sky
At night — 'twas little comfort there!

"Turn we, and try the longer round."
So spake his friends.—Ye patience lack;
A few brief hours, it may be found
'Twere best to have kept this shorter track.

And now the panting ice-blast sinks,
Before the all-conquering sun lies calm;
And lo! the rigid mountain drinks
From the soft vales the summer balm.

Then, scorning not the accustomed guide—
Spite dangers mountains always nurse—
Lo! safe he gains the other side,
And rests securely, none the worse.

Now mark! he sought no perilled track,
For want of patient waiting; nor
Baffled by obstacles, turned back;
Sure this was true Excelsior!

Now some start up with eager haste
(Who, waiting, might at length have won),
To perish on despair's chill waste,
Their aim unwrought, their course half run.

Ye who make haste to heap up gold—
Seize luring schemes, so seeming fair—
Tread slippery pathways, miss your hold,
And ruined fall, undone—beware!

Artists and authors! poets, too!
Who long to tread fame's flowery way;
Know, there's no open road for you;
None need so much, so oft to stay.

Though pseudo-friends may mock and jeer,
And prate of failure in delay,
Foretell defeat, call prudence fear—
None need so much, so oft to stay.

Aye, all who'd mount wealth's golden hill,
Or touch the topmost crags of fame,
Must, trained like soldiers, halt, stand still
At times, or they 'll ne'er reach the same.

When duty calls us, not to stay—
Then, pass we, spite all dangers, on!
But when mere rashness heads the way,
'Twere well to pause life's plains upon.

Ye labor well with arduous zeal,
Who see secure your crown at last:
But who can work and *wait*, and feel
Such barriers few have lived and past?

Toil then, scarce hoping for success;
Prepared stand out the iron gate;
It may be Heaven thy task may bless,
Time may uplift the bars of fate.

At least one work (we wait, 'tis true,
Some future its best worth to explain)
With this assurance comforts you:
That labor cannot be in vain.

DISMISS!

Some say there's no such thing in life—
That we can ne'er dismiss from duty—
We must be mingling 'mid earth's strife.
Aye, but from scenes of mirth, joy, beauty,
From friends we 've loved to have beside us,
From cheerful hours of cherished bliss—
Oh, these may be too soon denied us,
And we be summoned to "dismiss."

Commander Time his mandate sending,
Lo! General Change his will effects,
From rank to rank his stern way wending,
Performing all his lord directs.
And who so high, so blest in station,
Shall those unuttered edicts know—
Foretell his future occupation,
What he shall do, or whither go?

Some adverse winter warm hearts binding—
Lo! summer's sunshine breaks the spell!
And friends in prosperous hours are finding
They love no more, who once loved well!

Or, 'neath some chilling grief-mists shrouded,
Lo! vernal buds of hope arise;
Returns the sun of joy unclouded,
And floods with gems those tearful eyes!

Groups of the happy past conversing,
Called forth by Time to union sweet—
Now slowly year by year dispersing.
Till none shall soon be left to meet.
Perchance some quit earth's warlike regions,
Reposing in the land of peace;
And others unto distant legions
Are drafted—thus life's ranks decrease!

These last—still warriors—let them carry
The memory of each bivouac sweet,
Who with old friends were wont to tarry
Friends that they now no more can meet.
And, severed by Time's hurrying waters,
Let each one hold this maxim true:
We are but called to fresh head-quarters;
We 've still life's soldier-work to do.

FINIS.

CPSIA information can be obtained
at www.ICGtesting.com
Printed in the USA
LVHW100445110522
718424LV00003B/236

9 783375 001551